Heaven's Call

Second Edition

By Vanessa Haney

Dedication

To Mike, who gets out of bed before dawn to hike the desert with me and the howling coyotes. While I'm lost in my imagination, he marches quietly alongside to make sure I don't get murdered or try to pet a mountain lion. For this and a thousand other things, I am eternally grateful.

To Connor, who patiently sifts through the TikToks I send him and never says things like, "Aren't you supposed to be writing?"

To Sheri and Rebecca, who joined Kelly, Blanca, and Amanda as readers of my early drafts. Your opinions and your support are incredibly important to me. Oh, and, I should have mentioned this before but now that you're in Chuparosa, there's no escape.

.

Also by Vanessa Haney

Heaven's Lost (Book 1)
Heaven's Watch (Book 2)
Heaven's Call (Book 3)
The Chuparosa Chronicles (Short Stories)
The Devil's Memories (Book 4)

Prologue

The fallen angel known as Thomas prowled through a maze of tents that night on a surveillance mission of sorts.

By the end of October, the heat in Phoenix had finally abated enough that there were fewer daily deaths from exposure; but with no rain in weeks, a thick haze of dust and pollution hung in the air creating an additional layer of oppression in the atmosphere over The Zone.

The threat of extreme heat wouldn't come back for months, but the area between the state capitol and the court buildings where over a thousand unsheltered human beings lived on the streets remained infamous for overdoses and murder. Thomas was familiar with The Zone—not specifically, but from a thousand places he'd seen just like it all over the world, and the irreverence for life there irritated him.

At last, he found who he was looking for. That one soul in so much pain that the chance encounter with an angel from Hell might be the last, best thing to happen in his life. Though the night was not cold, the man shivered, clutching a camouflage backpack to his chest. His speech was rambling and as he rocked back and forth, his eyes pleaded with Thomas who could only guess what horrors the veteran had endured. The man's unspoken request was clear enough: give me anything to stop the pain.

Thomas pulled a packet of fentanyl-laced heroin from his jacket pocket and held it out to the young soldier. He had sourced it from a dog fighting cartel that dabbled in drugs on the side. He'd waited outside and unseen with a hideously deformed Pitbull named Carl, while the vampires Adam Colter and Cara Marshall tore through the warehouse arena. Thomas found Adam and his kind somewhat distasteful, but they were brutally efficient and when the screaming stopped, Thomas stepped over the gory remains of the dog handlers to gather the supplies he would need for his mission in The Zone.

As Thomas stared down at the desperate man, there was a prickling in his spine. He looked up and smiled as he felt a hand on his arm.

"Happy Halloween, brother."

Daniel's grip tightened on his arm. "Is this the best way to get information?"

"I'm told that around here, it's one of the only ways to get information."

"You'll kill him."

"You are content to watch him suffer then?" Thomas waved his hand across The Zone. "What if he is, quite justifiably, done living like this?"

"We are not the deciders of his fate."

Thomas jerked his arm free. "And you are not the

decider of mine."

"Who was the decider for James?" Daniel's eyes hardened, but his heart ached from the loss.

"You know the answer to that, you just won't admit it."

James was the angel once tasked with keeping Thomas in check and he had been Daniel's greatest friend. Daniel's last words to James had been, "I wish I could go with you," and he wondered every day if things would have been different had he followed his heart and done so.

"James was sent," he pressed his finger into Thomas's chest, "to keep you from exploiting more girls like Brona."

"First of all, she summoned me," Thomas said as he slapped Daniel's hand away. "Second, for years James and I enjoyed a wonderful game of cat and mouse until suddenly, his orders were to kill me. Why? Why would he go to Hell looking for me, Daniel? There was no way he could have been prepared for that journey." Thomas's eyes turned black, and his voice deepened with barely controlled outrage. "I was chained to the Rock while they tore him to shreds. He was ripped apart for blindly following orders."

In private, Daniel always questioned James's motivation. Not only had Thomas just confirmed his worst fears about his friend's death, but he had also given him cause to validate his own disobedience. Daniel was sent to kill Thomas's daughters, the Deane sisters, but instead he'd enlisted them and their powers to fight for him.

His only justification was that they were special to the Defenses he'd selected to be part of Heaven's

Watch. Heaven's Watch defended earth from restless beings who were even then plotting to take it from the humans. The humans who were regarded as the highest of all beings by the One who created them.

As such, his transgression had been overlooked, but he could see himself dancing on the same high wire as Thomas and was no longer confident to which side he would fall if the day ever came that he lost his balance.

The truth was that he'd always known the answer, he just didn't always know why. There was a line he would not cross, but he had to admit that the line had moved over the years. He would have to sit more with those thoughts and rather than dwelling on his reservations that night, he turned his attention to Thomas's appearance.

They'd both taken to dressing like average humans in dark blue jeans and casual button-down shirts. Nice enough to get into most places, but not so nice that they aroused suspicion. Even so, Thomas would have had a hard time fitting in anywhere but The Zone since the wounds he'd suffered when they fought weeks earlier were still oozing red. Even if he'd gone back to Hell, he should have had enough time to heal.

"Where have you been?" he asked.

"Confirming my theory."

Daniel was shocked. "I didn't think we could go to the Other Side."

"It's unpleasant, I'll give you that. But we can. I had to know exactly what would be coming after my children—besides you." Thomas suddenly grew tired, and his shoulders sagged. "It's Jaya, Daniel. She's alive and I called you here because she's coming for our people."

"No." Daniel shook his head in denial. He hadn't yet been created at the time, but he knew her story. "She was the last one to fall when the Nephilim fought one another. The flood wiped out most of the remaining Watchers and their children."

"Jaya was the only daughter. That woman clawed her way out of those raging waters, broke through the veil into the Other Side and has been waiting patiently for her moment ever since." Thomas smiled to himself. "And she's just a half-breed. Do you ever wonder if that's why we don't have sisters? Can you imagine the power?"

Daniel sneered. "If she's alive, then she's an abomination, like the rest of them. All of them."

"At least Laura and Sarah did not eat their mother," Thomas argued. "They may have been better off if they had, but chalk one up for evolution. In any case, you'd better take care of my little abominations because no one else can fight on Jaya's level."

"When she killed the troll, Laura sent a strong message to anyone thinking about following him through the veil. No matter how powerful Jaya is, those creatures are safe on the Other Side, and they'll hesitate to join her.

"True, but there are beings who have been banished to much darker places," Thomas knelt beside the soldier, who shrank away from his touch, "and it's places like this making them wake up and wonder how much longer the human reign can last."

The young man watched from the ground and listened to the angels as they argued. Though his body craved the contents of the pouch, he forced himself to consider the events that led him to that point in his life.

Complete recovery was an unclimbable hill; but in the moment, he felt it possible that if angels could find time to debate the value of his existence, maybe he could do one better and advocate for someone else's. At least until the Devil finally came to take him home.

Thomas dangled the pouch in front of him and asked, "Where can I find Nicholas Scott?" The young man clearly recognized the name, but refused to answer, so Thomas pulled back the drugs. "I heard he sees demons, does that ring a bell?"

The soldier pulled his knees to his chest and in a raspy voice said, "Everyone here sees demons, so leave that kid alone."

Thomas shrugged and said, "You'd better hope I find him before anything else does."

As he turned to leave, Daniel said, "I can't do my job if I have to question everything that I've always known to be true."

"Doubt is not necessarily rejection, Daniel. Sometimes it's growth."

Chapter One

When the banshee leaned its skinless, sunken skull over her bed, several strands of its coarse hair brushed across Sarah's face. In her sleep, she felt it hover but refused to acknowledge its presence. Her tossing and turning had awakened Drew and, fearing she'd come down with something, he placed the back of his hand against her forehead. Her skin was cool, but her breathing was labored, and she didn't respond when he shook her.

Just as he reached for his phone to call for help, her eyes flew open and she scrambled backward, spreading her arms wide to protect him. Flustered, he scanned the darkness until, at last, he could make out the faint outline of the banshee's gangly body crouching low near the bed. It caught him staring and every inch of his skin crawled as it stared back at him.

"What is that thing, Sarah?"

The spirit folded its hands on the pillow and rested its chin there, waiting for Sarah's acknowledgment but she pushed harder against Drew, crying, "You can't have him! It's a banshee, Drew, don't look at it!"

Well, crap. It was too late for that but if the creature was only a messenger, Drew hoped he might still have some time. It rose and took Sarah by the hand, tossing its other hand dismissively at Drew as it led her across the room and out the door. He followed them to the kitchen and found the love of his life standing nose to nose with the creature, staring it down.

"If not him, then who? Tell me!" Sarah demanded.

Awash with relief that he was not the next victim, Drew padded toward them, but Sarah held out her hand to stop him. She knew what was coming and though she knew it wouldn't block out the sound, covered her ears with her hands.

Drew clutched his chest when the banshee screamed. He'd never heard a sound so mournful and the longer it wailed the more his heart broke. He took Sarah into his arms and covered her hands with his own as if he could somehow lessen the pain for her.

The frames on the wall behind them began to rattle and pictures of her family and friends crashed to the tile at their feet. The front door swung open, and they clung to each other as the banshee drifted into the sunrise.

* * *

When Laura moved in with Sebastian, Sarah and Audi moved into her empty house. Everyone was happy with the new arrangements and, for the first time since they could remember, the Deane sisters were full of hope for the future. Hope that Laura would not allow to fade, even after learning of Sarah's visit from the banshee. She returned her phone to her back pocket, collected her drinks from the barista and set off to comfort Bash.

She would save the banshee news for later since he was already having a rough day.

Before they moved in together, she'd worried about the division of labor and expenses but having been single for so long, they both enjoyed cleaning, cooking, and shopping together. In fact, her newest favorite thing was watching him lose his mind at the self-checkout machine.

Once a month, they made a trip to Phoenix on a large grocery run and without fail, an item wouldn't scan, or he would have to wait for an assistant to check his identification for a bottle of wine. Further, it was awkward for him as the system wasn't designed for left-handed individuals. Rather than repeatedly explaining the economics of it, she had taken to wandering over to the coffee shop while he wrestled with the technology.

As she approached with their drinks, he scanned the eggs and leaned against the machine. "I don't fucking work here, Laura. Why do I have to do this?"

She eyed his body pressing on the scale and counted down in her head until it loudly complained, "Unrecognized item in the bagging area!"

"Jesus Christ!"

She stifled her laughter and pointed out that she had volunteered to do the scanning. Laura didn't like the new process either, but women were more accustomed to making the best of things.

He snatched the receipt from the dispenser, somehow tearing it in half lengthwise. "Eventually, I will beat this machine."

She kissed his cheek and handed him his drink. That the preferred caffeinated beverage of her rugged, cowboy sheriff turned out to be a cinnamon latte was another one of her new favorite things.

He sniffed at the lid and frowned. "The ones you make at home are better."

She took a long sip of her iced coffee and asked, "Are you going to complain about everything today?"

He chuckled and rubbed his goatee, embarrassed by how ridiculous he must look to her.

"No, I guess I'm done. Thank you, baby."

"For what?"

"For not letting me turn into a grumpy old man."

Once the groceries were put away at home, she reminded him of his promise to take her shopping, and he made a face, recalling the conversation about sheets. When Laura asked his opinion on redecorating their bedroom, he announced that he would happily sleep on sheets covered in Care Bears as long as he could sleep next to her. Though his sweet words earned him a blow job on the spot, they had not, evidently, gotten him out of a trip to the mall.

He did manage to put it off until after church so that Drew and Sarah could join them though. In the department store that anchored the mall, Sarah cheerfully selected bright colored curtains she'd always wanted but never bought because Rueben hated them.

She also picked out a throw pillow for Audi that read, "Don't make me drop a house on you." Audi's breakup with Noah had further strained the already tense relationship she had with her daughter, and she hoped some levity from their favorite season of American Horror Story would spark a conversation between the two of them.

Drew, however, was less pleased with the outing and glared at Bash over some sunflower covered towels that Sarah had piled in his arms. "You said this was going to be a double date for lunch in town."

Bash took the towels from him. "It is a double date, and we're gonna have lunch."

"The mall? My friend, you told a lie of omission."

Bash held up his hand in acknowledgement, "Alright, fine." Then he kissed Laura's cheek and held out his credit card. "Baby, we're going to Chuy's. Meet us in the bar when you get hungry."

She pursed her lips, looking from the card to his face and back. In the past, he would have angrily dismissed her reluctance to take it as stubborn and childish, but that day he held his hand steady while she worked through her decision. He'd fallen in love with a fiercely independent woman whom he desperately wanted to take care of and the differences in their personalities had nearly ruined their love affair on several occasions.

During his fatherless childhood, Bash developed certain opinions about how to be a good man and step one was to be the provider. Laura, however, had grown up believing that life was dangerous for a woman unable to provide for herself.

Deep down Bash knew that she would feel most cared for if he did something like weed her garden. The orders to her small tea business were pouring in and she had a lot of harvesting, drying, and packaging to do for her next batch. He was happy to weed and pay, but rather than pick a fight in Macy's, he offered his card, made a mental note to clear the garden, and left the rest up to her.

Laura supposed that since Bash hadn't cared about redecorating the bedroom and he certainly hadn't wanted to go to the mall, there was no reason he should have to pay for it. She'd figured out over time though that it would somehow be adding insult to injury if she didn't let him. So, while it made no sense to her, she took the card and smiled, saying, "We won't be too long."

The gravity of the one-minute subliminal exchange was not lost on their companions and Drew leaned close to Sarah, whispering, "I think we just witnessed some personal growth."

She winked at him as they walked away, and Bash noted how quickly Drew's spirits improved. He elbowed him with a sly grin and said, "Being in love suits you."

Drew picked up a candle labeled, "Peanut Butter Cookie" and corrected him, "Knowing she loves me back is what suits me." He brought the candle jar to his nose, inhaled deeply and gagged.

Bash threw his head back laughing, "Let's get out of here."

The restaurant was at the far end of the mall and while they walked, Bash quizzed Drew about the banshee. Loving a Deane witch included frequent, unsettling interactions with some of the darkest creatures the two men had ever come across. A banshee's warning was not to be dismissed and Bash was worried for them all.

"We're pretty sure it wasn't meant for me," Drew explained, "but just in case, I'm not going to waste any time with Sarah. We're too old for dating games anyway."

They found a high top for four in the bar and when their beers arrived Bash cautioned him, "Just don't make the same mistakes I did."

There were things in their past that Bash would never forgive himself for, but Laura had moved past them, and they were going to make it. Drew longed to be as rock solid in his own relationship but, for the time being, since he and Sarah had been so starved for affection, he was quite content with their honeymoon phase.

"I'm sure I'll make some of my own mistakes but right now, I'm busy having more sex than I've had in years."

Bash chuckled to himself, "I'm still catching up myself—my forties were dark."

"At our age, we only have a small window left for sex, so I plan to savor every bit of it."

"Aw hell," Bash ran a hand through his hair, "Daniel will get us killed before we're too old to do it anymore."

"Do you really think he'll let us die? Defenses can't be that easy to come by." Drew's thoughts returned to the banshee's warning.

Bash snapped his fingers. "Like that." There was a time when he thought like Drew, but he'd since come to believe that the only requirement for joining Heaven's Watch was significant emotional damage and there was plenty of that in Chuparosa. Daniel would only have to go down the street to replace them.

Drew disagreed with his friend. Even if anyone could do it, he doubted that very many would. Saving the argument for another day, he steered the conversation back to Sarah.

"You know she never..." he briefly reconsidered bringing it up, but there was no one he trusted more than Bash, so he continued, "she never had a say in it, and now we're trying to figure out what she even likes in bed."

Bash made a face, but rather than speak ill of Rueben, he tipped his beer bottle at Drew. "That's the best kind of investigation." He thought for a moment and added, "Laura reads some pretty dark romance, but I don't think she wants to actually *do* any of that stuff. She bites me though, so I guess I should probably ask her."

"She bites you?"

"Not there."

"Oh. Well, I'll dress up like Tarzan if Sarah wants me to but—"

Bash winced. "Thanks for that mental image."

They sat in silence for a while and watched the baseball game until Drew couldn't help himself from asking, "Where does she bite you?"

Bash smirked and took another sip of his beer, but before he could reply, two gunshots rang out from across the mall.

Laura and Sarah had been browsing Hot Topic when the first shots were fired and dropped instantly to the floor under a rack of teddy bear hoodies. The teenager at the cash register dug frantically through a drawer for the key to lower the security gate while screams echoed through the mall as people ran for the exits. Laura motioned for the girl to get down and rubbed her hands together, sparking some static electricity.

"We can't get stuck in here." She told Sarah.

They crouched low, made their way to the front of

the store and hid behind a display of Sailor Moon pajamas. "Those shots were close," Sarah noted as she poked her head around the display, "but I don't see him."

"Wait, what the hell is that?"

Something tall and thin with arms so long they dragged the floor ran down the mall towards the Hot Topic, followed closely by a man in a blue flannel shirt waving a pistol.

"Stop!" he shouted at the thing and fired but missed his target, exploding a display of ceramic pins behind the women.

Sarah crawled to the girl cowering under the cash register and whispered, "Where's the back room?"

She followed the girl's gaze about fifty feet behind the counter to a door covered in heavy metal posters. The man fired another shot into the store, and they covered their heads as the light fixture shattered down on them from above. The girl screamed, and they looked up to find the creature hovering with its long arms pressed into the countertop. It leaned over and opened its mouth wide, exposing sharp teeth and a long, spiked tongue. Sarah raised her arms and used her mind to throw it across the store.

She hissed, "Go now. Stay low," and the girl bolted for the back door. When it slammed behind her, Sarah grabbed Laura by the shoulders and pushed her under the counter. "We've got a big problem."

Chapter Two

Bash and Drew dove off their stools and crawled into the mall just as the security gate came down behind them. "He's taken three shots with a pistol," Bash said. "Let's hope that's the only weapon he's got."

Drew pulled out his phone. "They could be anywhere right now."

Bash stopped him from dialing. "They'll have their phones turned off."

It was true. Sarah taught middle school for twenty years and Laura spent as much time working in government buildings downtown. Between the two of them, they'd endured dozens of active shooter drills and had silenced their phones as soon as they found shelter in the store.

Though it was the beginning of November, Christmas shoppers were spending more time online, and since the mall was partially vacant, it hosted a smaller than usual Sunday crowd. Most people had already escaped through the exits and the few who remained were huddled in small masses, making their way to the restaurant. Drew motioned for the bartender to open the gate, and he raised it enough for them to get to safety. There was more shouting from a few stores away and another shot was fired. Bash put a finger to his lips and waved the people inside.

"Quickly." Drew pushed the last person under the gate as it crashed closed. He gave the bartender a thumbs up and crouched low next to Bash. "What are you thinking?"

"Are you armed?"

"Yeah."

"Keep it holstered unless you need it so you don't get shot by the cops when they get here."

Just then a young security guard bounded around the corner, knocking Bash over. No more than twenty-one years old, the guard's eyes were wide, and his face was flushed with excitement. He grabbed Bash by the arm and helped him to his feet. "Don't worry, sir. I'll get you out of here."

"Get off me." Bash jerked away from him.

Drew covered a smile with his hand. "He's just a kid trying to do his job."

"I didn't think I would need this today," Bash dug his badge out of his pocket and clipped it to his belt, "but it's alright kid, I'm deputy sheriff Sebastian Scott." He nodded at Drew, "This is my uh...partner, Andrew Clarke." He tapped the radio hanging on the guard's belt. "Any word from the police?"

The young man shook his head. "This radio never works, and they make me turn in my cell phone before I start my shift." He stuck his hand out, "My name's Todd, by the way."

Bash frowned. "Well, listen Todd, the shots are

coming from about three doors down. We've got people over there and we're gonna go get them. We'll need your help if there are wounded. Are you up for that?"

"Yes, sir."

"What have you got? A gun? A taser?"

Todd shook his head again. "I'm not supposed to have it but there's pepper spray in my pocket."

"Are you fucking kidding me?"

Drew laid a hand on the young man's shoulder and asked, "What exactly is your job, son?"

"Never mind. Look at me." Bash punched the kid lightly on the arm. "Pay attention and don't get shot today, alright?"

In the distance, they heard Laura shout, "Let her go!"

Drew's heart thumped so loud he could barely hear his own voice. "He must have Sarah."

"Not for long." Bash drew his pistol and the three of them ran down the mall.

The gangly creature popped out of the corner, grabbed Sarah from behind and dragged her to the middle of the mall. Its limbs were thin but strong and the more she struggled, the tighter its grip.

Laura flicked the phosphorescent paint on her fingernails and filled her hands with fire. "I said let her go."

Her eardrums rattled then when behind her, the shooter raised his pistol and fired into the ceiling. Whirling on him, Laura shrieked, "Put that thing away right now!"

He eyed the fire in her hands and took a step backward aiming his gun at her chest. "Demons everywhere."

"Oh, my god." Sarah rolled her eyes and let her head fall back onto the creature's chest. "Not us, pal."

Laura held up her hands. "Just put the gun down and let us deal with this."

"No way."

"He fears you," the creature said. It stroked Sarah's hair with its free hand, tugging hard on the ends. "But I don't...witch."

"Let me..." Laura's mind raced. Even if she used magic, he would probably shoot again before she could disarm him; and he was a bad enough shot that he was more likely to kill Sarah than her. "Let me help my sister."

He stepped backward into a planter and pulled the trigger as he stumbled. Laura rolled her eyes as the bullet hit the glass case surrounding the pretzel shop. Sarah used her mind to shove him into the White Barn and with one hand Laura threw a stream of fire, lighting every candle in the place with flames as tall as they could go. With her other hand she draped a net of electricity over the creature, using just enough power to hold it there since it still had Sarah.

Bash could think of nothing but the banshee's warning as he ran through the mall trying to convince himself that Laura couldn't die, not after all they'd been through. He and the others came to a screeching halt in front of the candle store, startling the shooter who fired again, knocking down a shelf of wax warmers.

Bash aimed his revolver, but Laura screamed, "Don't kill him, Bash! He's after this thing!"

He jumped out of the way as Todd dove into the White Barn, tackling the shooter and showering them both with pepper spray.

Out of nowhere they heard, "Laura Deane, you will stand down!"

Bash would recognize that booming voice anywhere and a fresh wave of fear flowed into his heart.

Laura moved closer to Sarah as six non-uniformed officers stormed in, wrestling the shooter and the security guard away. "Bash, what's happening?"

He raised his hands over his head and several more officers surrounded them. "Hold it baby, don't move."

Samuel Parker approached them casually. He was a tall, official-looking black man with a pistol on his hip that, even in all the excitement, he hadn't bothered to draw.

"What's your plan, sweetheart?" he asked Laura.

Laura looked from him to Sarah and back. "I'm not letting it go."

"If you're smart," Samuel drawled, "you won't even let it live."

Laura was unwilling to attack as long as it had her sister, but Sarah locked eyes with her and said, "It will be okay if I disappear."

Samuel was unsure of what she meant by that and was ready to intervene, but Bash and Drew each took a step backward so he followed their lead, waving at his men to do the same. He'd worked with Sebastian enough in the past to trust his instincts.

The creature held her arms at her sides so Sarah couldn't reach the crystal that hung around her waist, but she stilled her breath and let her eyes flutter closed as she concentrated. She hadn't used the invisibility spell since they'd defeated Fiona and the troll, but she called it up in her mind and her body tingled as the clear quartz awakened and warmed her skin.

She could not truly become transparent but the glass surrounding the shops in the mall reflected so brightly that the others became disoriented and lost sight of her. The creature turned its head and loosened its grip just enough for her to kick backward, blowing out its knee with a sickening crunch.

"Now!"

The distracted men regained their focus and when the creature buckled, Drew pulled Sarah away from it.

Laura advanced then, tightening the cage of electricity around it. Bash gave her a nod, so she flicked her fingernails and dropped a stream of fire into the thing until it stilled and smoldered at her feet.

Samuel stepped over it and held out his hand. "Sebastian Scott. You're looking well-fed for once. How've you been?" He eyed Laura up and down and winked at Bash. "Go big or go home, eh?" Laura narrowed her eyes at him, so he added, "Paranormally speaking, of course."

Crowded into the administrative office of the mall, the shooter lay unconscious on the floor and Todd slumped in the corner, eyes running from the pepper spray. Drew and Sarah hung back by the door while Bash and Samuel spoke quietly behind the desk and Laura sat with her legs crossed primly in the guest chair, glaring at them both.

"Who are you? What was that thing? And, how do you know who I am?" she demanded.

"I'll explain it to you later, baby."

"You will explain it to me now, Sebastian."

"I'll get you out of the shit, my friend," Samuel laughed and slapped Bash on the back. "I am Special Inspector Samuel Parker—you can call me Sam."

Drew leaned forward. "Special Inspector?"

"Once upon a time, Bash and I hunted the kinds of bad guys that require more...specialized attention."

Everyone knew that after the Army, Bash worked in the Phoenix office of the Sheriff's Department for several years before moving to Chuparosa, and that he met Chuck on an unusual assignment that frequently took them all over the state. However, the nature of that assignment was not commonly known, nor did anyone understand the toll it had taken on the men.

One of the incredible things about their state was that a person could drive two hours in any direction and go from a sweltering desert to the breezy cool pines, and in two hours more be in the badlands of the petrified forest. Arizona's magical landscape hosted any number of supernatural elements and if you weren't paying attention, one trip through Sedona could land you in another dimension.

Over time, the Sheriff's Department created a special unit charged with keeping those elements in line, inasmuch as that was possible. From their own ranks they quietly recruited officers who were, for one reason or another, best suited for the job. Chuck's connection to Chuparosa made him uniquely qualified and Sebastian just never fit in anywhere else.

The picture was clearing up for Drew who remembered the one monster his friend feared the most. "You hunted vampires."

"Among other things," Sam nodded. "Chuck used to come along for the ride every now and then—how's he doing?"

"That wasn't a vampire in the mall," Drew pressed.

"*That* was an Inhabitor Gremlin. They move into buildings that are dying, like this half-empty mall and usually prey on the staff until it closes up. Halloween was a few days ago so he probably poked through the veil that night. He would have lived here hurting people and breaking shit until the place fell down around his ears."

"What then?" Drew asked.

"Gremlins aren't that forward thinking." Sam gestured at the unconscious shooter. "When our hero called 911 about a *demon* on the loose, he was told to leave it alone, evacuate and let the authorities handle it. Instead, he decided to go all Wyatt Earp on us, and now, here we are."

Drew was fascinated. "You were a special inspector, too?"

Bash shook his head and Sam clarified, "He could have been, but he moved out to the boonies instead. I suppose being strung up in a vampire nest for a couple days is hard on a man, and I'll tell you what, it was quite a fight. Bash was a mess but, uh," Sam smiled big, "you should have seen the other guys."

Drew paled. That Bash had even spoken to Adam was a miracle.

Sam's eyes settled on Laura. "Looks like Chuparosa's been good to him though."

Noting the look on Laura's face, Bash took her hand and gave it a squeeze. "I told you all about my old job."

It was true, but she didn't relax. "Why does he know

so much about me?"

Bash raised his eyebrows at his old friend. They hadn't seen each other in a long time, and he wanted to know the answer to that question himself.

"I had a few run-ins with Fiona," Sam explained, "and over the years, the Deane family has become something of a hobby of mine."

Bash looked at Laura, "I didn't know that."

"It's all good. I watched the kids scuttle her trailer up north and I've got no beef with you or your sister...at this time."

Bash tightened his jaw. "You had our kids under surveillance?"

"Purely coincidental," Sam said, "they didn't know it, but they were doing me a huge favor."

The shooter made a gurgling noise and Bash squared his shoulders. "What are we gonna do about him?"

Sam pulled a business card from his shirt pocket and handed it to the security guard. "You're pretty good in a fight so give me a call if you want a new job."

Sarah took a pencil from the desk, rubbed the eraser back and forth several times and collected the shavings in her palm. Crouching in front of the shooter, she blew the shavings into his face and murmured, "Forget me now, forget what you saw, forget what was said here, forget it all."

Bash leaned over him. "Are you alright now, sir?"

The man blinked a few times and looked around the room. "Where am I?"

"You're in the office." Sam hauled him to his feet. "I would get a medical professional to check that out if I were you."

"Check what out?"

Sarah opened the door for him and handed him a bottle of water. "It's probably just dehydration, but you never know."

Focused more on his mysterious health problem than his missing gun, the shooter staggered into the hallway. "I will. Of course, I will. Thank you."

When he was gone, Sam turned to Bash. "Are you going to invite me over so we can catch up?"

Laura folded her arms across her chest and Bash said, "Nope."

Chapter Three

Mena Ruiz paced in her kitchen like a caged animal until Laura answered her call. "So, I guess we can't take you anywhere now." Her tone was joking, but she'd been absolutely terrified for her best friend when Chuck relayed Bash's story about the active shooter in the mall.

It would have done no good to try to ease Mena's mind, so Laura gave her account of the events and pressed ahead, adding the private concerns she had from the day. "What do you know about Samuel Parker?"

Mena groaned with annoyance. "Besides how Chuck almost died every time they worked together?"

Chuck's dangerous special assignments came to an end when he took over as lead deputy sheriff in Chuparosa; but when their kids were little Laura sat with Mena on many nights as she worried for her husband.

"I never met the man and it's a good thing. For him."

"There's nothing you remember at all?"

Mena thought for a moment, "I remember Chuck

saying he had three ex-wives, but no kids."

"Well, you don't have to tell me how hard it is when the supernatural gets involved in a relationship."

"Against my better judgment, I do feel bad for him sometimes," Mena agreed, "and in his defense, Chuck says he is entirely devoted to keeping people safe...ish."

Mena's house was buzzing with so much activity that night, Laura could barely hear her over the phone.

"Are you having a party?"

Audra Deane was spending the night with Mena's daughter. Their good friend, Boone, had brought over his cat, Oliver, to cheer her up as they analyzed Audi's recent breakup with Noah.

Mena moved closer to the back door, lowering her voice. "We need to talk about Audi."

Laura had known that her niece was struggling but the breakup was stunning. Audi might have taken in stride the revelation that her family was part angel and the deadly responsibilities that came with being one of Heaven's Watch, had they not instantly resulted in her kidnapping, her father's death, and the near execution of her mother.

Audi shared the family's cynicism and coped by using dark humor but also like the rest of them, she tended to withdraw. Noah would only be the first in a long line of abandoned loved ones if they couldn't save her from herself.

Audi's mother knew this better than anyone, but Sarah was hesitant to offer advice lest she look like a hypocrite. She'd almost gotten herself killed by cutting off everyone she loved and was at a loss over how to keep her daughter from repeating her mistakes. Things between them had improved a bit since they moved into

Laura's house and they had fun making over the place, but the relationship strained anew whenever she tried to talk about Noah.

As Audi faced the reality that everyone she knew was in perpetual danger, letting Noah go before the world lost him for good made more sense to her. What she hadn't considered was that his involvement with the rest of her family wasn't up to her and he made that plain when they broke up. It had come down to whether or not she would admit that she wanted him in her life and how long he would wait to see if she did.

Laura and Mena listened in without shame as Tina Ruiz and her friends took over the kitchen table.

"It was just a small fight," Audi explained, "and then it was a hurricane and then he was gone." Her lip quivered but she refused to cry, adding stubbornly, "I don't know who he thinks he is. It's too dangerous around us when shit hits the fan," she tipped an imaginary cowboy hat, "but he wants to be like Sheriff Scott so bad."

Boone dangled a string over Oliver's head. "Who wouldn't want to be like Sheriff Scott?"

Audi scoffed, "Sheriff Scott doesn't even want to be like Sheriff Scott."

Tina sighed inwardly at the mention of her secret crush, but she had to admit that Sebastian's life expectancy was fairly low, even for a law enforcement officer. So, though she believed Audi was wrong, Tina would stick by her best friend, delicately pleading Noah's case from time to time.

"He doesn't just love you. He wants to be part of what you do."

Mena put her hand over the speaker, suggesting

quietly, "Do you think we could get them into counseling?"

"That's not the worst idea. I'll give David Trainer a call. He works for the government, but he knows all about us and he might agree to take on a private client." Laura paused for a second and added, "I just thought of something else that could work even better though. I'll talk to you soon." She hung up and dialed Brian's number.

Chuck strode though the kitchen just then wearing basketball shorts and a long t-shirt. Eyeing the young people at the table, he pulled Mena aside. "Did I miss a memo?"

"We're not invited to this meeting." Mena smiled and handed him a giant water bottle.

News of Audi's breakup was, of course, all over town, but Chuck happened to hear the story from Bash, who was there when Audi showed up in hysterical tears the night it happened. He and Chuck decided that Noah's heart had been collateral damage from one of the wildest years of their lives, and though they felt bad for him, they weren't at all surprised.

At that moment, Chuck was more concerned about the reappearance of Samuel Parker. He was sure it was coincidence that Bash ran into him during the incident at the mall, but Chuck knew they had never left Sam's radar and he didn't want their old boss getting any ideas. Their hands were full enough.

So as not to pile on to Audi's worries, he lowered his voice before asking Mena, "How's Laura doing?"

"She's probably making a list of abandoned buildings nearby and planning to clear out all the Inhabitor Gremlins. I had no idea that was even a thing."

Mena offered him a granola bar, but he shook his head. "Honestly Chuck, we deal with so much that you would think we could go shopping in peace."

"Well, I hate to say it," Chuck folded her into his arms, "but it's a good thing they were there."

She knew he wished he'd been there too, and she relaxed into him, grateful that he wasn't. Their marriage struggled for survival early on when Chuck was away for weeks at a time. They'd rallied, but some stagnant years slipped by them when Tina was in high school.

Since she graduated, they had been enjoying a much-needed refresh and Mena jealously guarded their relationship as if it were the holy grail because, to her, it was. She didn't completely share in his optimism but after nearly thirty years of marriage, she trusted his intuition almost as much as she trusted her own.

"My Mena," he nuzzled her ear and caressed her back, "we'll take care of each other." She gave him a doubtful smile, so he backed her against the sink for a long, wet kiss.

Tina made a gagging noise and Boone curled his lip. "How is it that these old people are getting more action than me?"

"Who's old, punk?" Chuck tossed him the basketball and they played keep away from Oliver for a few minutes.

When Chuck finally headed out, Mena called after him, "Don't forget your knee brace!" He gave her the thumbs up and closed the door.

On Tuesday evenings when the weather cooled, the

men in town often played pickup basketball games on the court outside of the YMCA. They played on weeknights as opposed to weekends so as not to be invasive to the kids and, more recently, so that Adam wouldn't get incinerated by the sun.

Chuck found Bash and Watson wrestling nearby on one of the only patches of grass in town. The enormous German Shepherd was a well-behaved and vigilant protector but given his size, questionable provenance and the unpredictable circumstances they frequently found themselves in, Bash had lately been experimenting with some more formal training techniques.

Weeks earlier, he started with a ball and a treat to hold Watson's attention, then graduated to hand signals and finally Chuck had to look hard for the almost imperceptible cues that Bash used to get the dog into fighting position. Watson knew from experience that his *big man* would take care of him, so he patiently endured the training and memorized the commands. He also knew that Bash couldn't help himself after too long and could look forward to playing ball and rolling around when they got bored with the training.

"You're gonna wear yourself out before the game, man."

Chuck heaved his friend up and gave Watson a vigorous scratch around the collar. While the men chatted, a jackrabbit popped its head from behind a bush and Watson grew very still, staring it down. Laura had taught the dog not to chase rabbits because in Chuparosa a fair number of them would chase back—and bite. In addition to his astonishing self-control, she and Bash suspected that the hellhound had plenty of other powers and wished he could talk about them.

For his part, Watson was delighted with his new parents. Bash and Laura showered him with affection and their lifestyle regularly gave him the opportunity to act on his baser instincts. He was just as likely to be able to tear apart a monster as he was to run after birds, and he was happy either way.

Adam and Drew joined them on the court that night with Benjamin Bradford. Ben was the good natured, thirty-year-old assistant pastor at the nondenominational church on the edge of town. His fiancé had ended their engagement a few weeks prior and though Ben's heart was shattered, the other men suspected that she'd broken up with Chuparosa more than she'd broken up with him. Small town life, particularly theirs, was not for everyone and she'd had a problem fitting in from the beginning.

His father was a burly carpenter named Jack and they'd moved into the old Lancaster place when Ben was nine years old. Their arrival was a curious event that raised a lot of questions since Ben was in a cast from his shoulder to his wrist at the time. Long after he was grown the town still speculated about how the boy might have broken his arm.

For a while, Jack was the unofficial suspect but that seemed unlikely since he doted so tenderly on his son. The coffee klatch eventually decided that since Ben was so active, his injury must have been an accident. A story went around town that his mother died and that a small-town environment was preferable to Phoenix for raising a boy alone, although it was universally acknowledged that Chuparosa was an odd choice.

Ben once confided in Drew that alcoholism was the

real culprit. Jack came home one night to find his son cradling his arm on the front porch steps and his wife passed out on the living room floor. Ben had crashed his bike on the way home from school, but his mother was too drunk to understand so he waited outside and tried to be brave.

Jack broke down in the emergency room and promised his little boy that he would "get off his ass and fix everything." True to his word, they stayed in a motel room that night and Ben rarely saw his mother after that. A few years later, Jack married a kindergarten teacher who introduced them to church, defining the course of Ben's life forever.

"Let's wait a few minutes in case someone else shows up," he said to the others.

Ben was taking over for the head pastor who was on vacation, and he'd invited several men from his congregation to play. Drew appreciated the younger man's acceptance of them but was pretty sure he knew why no one else had come out.

"Do you think it's wise to be seen with us, Ben?" He pulled off his t-shirt and called out, "Skins!"

Bash pulled off his shirt as well, adding, "Everyone's a faithful servant until they find out that there's real live angels running around the place recruiting volunteers."

Chuck laughed. "The likes of us, no less."

Eyeing the numerous scars across their bodies, Ben was surprised by the lack of resentment in the tone behind their jokes. He supposed that, in the end, it didn't make sense for men who lived on borrowed time to waste it being bitter. Their casual acceptance of the unimaginable job they'd been given was inspiring, but he kept them at the top of his prayer list all the same.

"They can judge," he grinned, "but I exist only to play ball and save souls."

"You've got your work cut out for you in this group, Preacher." They spun around to see Sam standing at the edge of the court, dressed to play, and spinning a ball between his hands. "Looks like you need one more—or do you keep the kid around to rotate in when one of you geezers get tired?"

"Call me Sam. I met Andrew a few days ago," he said for Adam's and Ben's benefit, "but I go way back with these two." Sam noted that while Ben stuck out his hand and introduced himself, Adam hung back and only nodded a greeting.

"Yep," Bash snarked, "I even shot him once."

Ben's eyes widened, but Chuck tapped his wristwatch, "Are we talking or playing?"

Bash swiped the ball from Sam and made a three pointer so the Skins, rounded out with Adam, took possession and headed down the court. The game was friendly at first, if lively, with Watson running alongside, barking out his support for each basket, regardless of the scoring team.

But then the fouls between Sam, Chuck, and Bash started to get a little rougher. Things got out of hand when Chuck shoulder-checked Sam to the cement, so the others dropped out one by one to give them room for a more combat-style game.

"I'm afraid they're working through something that we, thank God, will never truly understand," Drew said and flopped onto a bench, taking a long swig from his water bottle.

"I don't know," Adam disagreed, "I believe you

understand quite a bit, yourself."

Ben wiped his face with the bottom of his t-shirt. "There will be high places in Heaven for all of you."

Drew's expression turned grim, and he said, "I'm told that's not how it works."

Chapter Four

Given the aggressiveness of their play, it was no wonder that an accident ended the game. Sam stumbled into Bash, knocking the wind out of both of them as they hit the concrete. Watson intervened with a warning growl directed at the new guy and Bash did his best to reassure the dog as well as everyone else, wheezing, "It's okay boy, we're just playing around."

Adam and Drew weren't convinced but kept their comments to themselves. Once everyone sprawled on the grass, exhausted but finally unwound, Watson gave Sam a sniff. He did his best to remain still and made a mental note to keep treats on him when he visited Chuparosa. "Where in the hell did you get this enormous dog?"

"I'm not sure which zip code he comes from down there." Bash looked at Drew, "Did Thomas ever tell you?"

"Hey, about this Thomas..." Sam decided to pursue Watson's origins at a later time and seized on the mention of the mystery man he'd been trying to find since the kids up north mentioned him.

Bash shook his head and rolled onto his back. "Never mind. I'm not talking about him tonight."

Bash wasn't going help him with the Thomas puzzle, but he'd said enough to give Sam some pieces to put together, which was more than he had before. Further, if his old friend had gone through an ordeal that allowed him to acquire an actual hellhound, that explained a few other significant details.

He tapped Bash playfully with his fist and gave a nod in Adam's direction. "Since when?"

That Sebastian had allowed a vampire within a day's drive of him without burning up the entire town was a notion that just three years ago would have been absurd.

Bash rubbed unconsciously at the faded fang marks on his forearm. He had been wondering how long it would take for Sam to figure Adam out. He'd always had an uncanny gift for identifying creatures of all kinds and surely made him for a vampire right away.

Adam held his breath, but he needn't have worried because without hesitation Bash said, "Adam is a friend."

"Well, I'll be damned. I'd like to say that now I've seen everything," he said, leaning back on his elbows, "but we all know that's probably not the case."

The sheriff's deputies laughed but the pastors could feel the emotional temperature of each man go cold, and Ben could not resist asking, "Were you serious, Bash? When you said you shot him?"

Bash shrugged and tossed him a Gatorade. He had told a somewhat sanitized account of their last adventure at the mall, but since they were away from mixed company and, apparently, among friends, Sam began with the full version.

"A few years ago, we tracked a couple of vampires nesting in a cave just outside of the Fort Apache Indian Reservation, near Pinetop," he paused to let them take that in, adding, "you see, they're afraid to go on the reservation, but they like those wide-open spaces with lots of privacy and those caves were perfect. Present company excluded, I'm sure," he gave Adam a nod, "but most vampires like to torture you a while before, well...you know.

"During the fight, they threw Chuck against the wall of that cave so hard that we thought for sure he was dead, just lying there all broken in the dirt. One had Bash on the ground and the other had me by the throat and," he laughed strangely, as if there were memories of the experience that still surprised him, "my feet didn't even touch the ground."

Ben gasped. These were big men—strong and violent. They'd faced powerful forces that no one could ever adequately prepare for, and they would do it until they died. Even the games they played took on an air of life and death. It was what they knew to do when they were together, like muscle memory. His dear friend, Andrew, had been drawn into their work as well and he feared for them all.

"Anyway," Sam continued, "it was scratching at me with those nails, just playin' like they do."

Ben and Drew noticed the slash marks peeking out from the neck of his shirt and gave each other nervous looks.

"But here's where it gets crazy: they didn't think to disarm us in the fight because bullets don't do nothin' to 'em. So, I reminded Bash that they can't drink blood from a dead man and this asshole don't even take two seconds to think about it—he just shoots me right then and there. That blood sucker was so pissed, he tossed me over the cliff like a bag of trash but," he laughed again, "it turns out there was plenty of cactus to slow me down as I fell.

"I give Bash a hard time, but he's the best shot I know, and he got me low in the shoulder, not quite the heart. It hurt like a bitch," he glared at Bash half-heartedly, "but I figured that if the fall didn't kill me first, I'd probably be okay in the end. All things considered."

"He saved your life...by shooting you." Ben was in awe.

"Make no mistake," Sam clarified, "that night, I would have been saved even if that shot was fatal."

Bash could still recall how desperate and alone he felt when the vengeful vampires turned on him. He shifted uncomfortably on the grass as his hips began to throb with phantom pain. They'd tied him by the ankles and nearly pulled his legs off, hanging him upside down from the mouth of the cave.

"It was almost dawn," he remembered aloud, "and that's what really saved us all."

The vampires left him hanging there with promises of how slowly he was going to die and went deep inside the cave to avoid the light. While they slept, Bash tried for hours to free himself, but the knots were too tight. He was exhausted and woozy and his nose had started to bleed and just when he began to pray for a massive stroke, he noticed a tall, dead saguaro a few feet away.

It took several tries, but he swung his body and grabbed hold of the cactus, breaking long ribs off the skeleton and stuffing them into his belt. After gathering a handful, he heard a weak voice from below.

"Bash, what are you doing?" Chuck was alive, but barely.

Sebastian tossed him a couple of cactus ribs and whisper-yelled, "You still got your gun?"

Chuck didn't answer but his eyes were open, so Bash told him the plan. "They'll be awake soon. Listen, if I can't pull this off, you blow my fucking brains out, you understand? Don't let them take me...and don't let them take you, either."

Chuck closed his eyes and Bash couldn't tell if he'd understood or not, but he made sure he was ready when the first vampire came forward at sunset.

"What's going on here?" With a confused look, it poked at him as he clung, still upside down, to the dead cactus. Bash gave it no time to think, pushing off and stabbing it as he swung through the air. It bellowed in pain and crumpled next to Chuck, who rose up and ran it through again with one of the ribs Bash gave him. He swiped a small machete from the vampire's belt and though it was an agonizing, slow crawl, managed to get it to Bash before collapsing.

Bash cut himself free and crashed down to the hard dirt. The pain was awful, and his legs would twitch now and then as the feeling returned to them, but he laid there as still as he could be. The second vampire emerged howling with rage and lunged for him, but Bash used its momentum and the last of his strength to impale it.

When Sam clawed his way back up the cliffside, he found Bash crouched in the corner next to Chuck. They were both muttering and covered in blood and there were pieces of vampire scattered all over the cave. Bash clutched the last of his cactus ribs until the paramedics sedated him and since then he always kept that small machete in his truck.

"My God," Drew whispered.

Sam eyed Adam suspiciously and said, "You're awful quiet."

Adam had tracked those vampires himself for close to six months and he'd just sorted out a long, unsolved mystery by listening to their story.

"I knew of those Pinetop vampires," he said coldly. "They toyed with someone I cared very much about. You must have gotten to them right before me because I saw the aftermath, though I never found..." his voice trailed off as a moment of grief scattered his thoughts.

The others leaned in, thinking they might get another glimpse into Adam's past, but he wasn't ready to talk about it and collected himself quickly.

"Anyway, I'm sorry for what you went through, but I'll be forever grateful for what you did. I am particularly pleased to learn that they died so...painfully."

"Well, now you know that a dead saguaro rib will work just as well as any wooden stake," Sam warned, "so, mind yourself."

* * *

Laura was in the kitchen when she heard his truck pull in the driveway. She hid the tray she'd been putting together with no time to spare before Bash came bounding through the back door with Watson at his heels.

"There's our Laura!"

Watson nudged her knees and Bash pulled her into a bear hug.

"Ew," she joked, wriggling out of his sweaty embrace, "what put you two in such a good mood?"

He leaned into the refrigerator and dug around for a snack. "I'm just happy to be alive, baby."

She paused and studied him carefully. He didn't elaborate, so evidently that sentence was meant to be taken at face value; but it made her nervous when he talked like that, tempting fate. His spirit was light though, and she wanted to keep it that way.

"Go shower," she waved him off to the bathroom, "and I'll fix you something."

He gathered her to him again, pressing their hips together, "I'll fix *you* something."

She pushed him away, laughing, "Go."

After filling Watson's dishes and giving him some love, she returned to her work. It was a risk as Bash might have been too tired after the basketball game, but she'd planned a romantic evening, arranging a tray filled with fruit and cheese next to a bottle of wine on the dresser in their bedroom. His melodramatic groaning as the hot shower massaged his muscles let her know she had plenty of time and it also made her smile.

Since she'd started watching him go about his day-to-day activities, she found that even though he fought monsters with her, she loved the ordinary, silly things he did the most. He had no idea how her heart swelled when she found him asleep on the couch ten minutes into a baseball game, or when she caught him swiping strawberries from the garden. At first it drove her bananas that he smacked her backside every time he walked by, but she wouldn't survive a week if he ever stopped.

She poured two glasses of wine, lit candles all around the room and turned down the bed. When the water shut off in the bathroom, she hurried into his favorite nightgown. It was emerald green with a white lace bodice and spaghetti straps. There was a zipper in front that went to her navel and the hem fell just above her knees.

He emerged from the bathroom in a cloud of steam with a towel around his waist. He didn't see her at first, but his lips crept into a smile as he scanned the room and made his way to the dresser. Popping a piece of cheese into his mouth, he grinned into the candlelight.

"What's all this about?"

She stepped around the closet door and asked, "How tired are you tonight?"

He gave her no answer, but he was across the room in three steps, sliding his hands along the fabric of the gown. "Mmm...silky...sexy..." He pushed her hair aside and nibbled at her neck. "Damn, woman." He squeezed her bottom and brought her lips to his.

As they kissed, he pulled on the zipper and slipped his hand inside the gown. "You are so fucking beautiful."

When he swept her up, she nuzzled his ear, whispering, "I like it when you carry me."

"Well," his voice was thick with passion as he brought her to the bed, "I like to lay you down."

He left a trail of kisses down her body and pushed the nightgown up over her hips. She made a soft noise as he dipped his head between her legs for what he liked to do most. As his tongue swirled and drove her to the brink, she buried her hands in his hair and cried out his name. He loved to hear that and smiled to himself as her body shook from the pleasure, thinking he might give it another go.

Before he got the chance, she pushed him onto his back, purring, "Can I ride you?"

"Hell yeah, you can."

He pressed his hands up her thighs and arched his hips as she eased herself onto him. The straps of the gown fell over her shoulders and as they found their rhythm, she brought his fingers to her mouth, sucking lightly on his thumb.

His body tensed and he groaned, "God Laura, you move so good."

"Just a little more?" She breathed, "Sebastian, please?"

"Take your time, baby."

He bit the inside of his cheek, hoping he hadn't over promised. But when he skimmed his wet thumbs over her nipples, her head fell back and she pushed her hands into his chest, crying out for him again. He rose up clinging to her, kissing her lips and neck and as he rolled her onto her back, she bit down on his shoulder.

"Ow," he gasped, grabbing a fistful of hair on the back of her head, "I love it when you do that."

She wrapped her legs around him and he lost control, thrusting hard and growling incoherently as he came.

As his body relaxed, she gently raked her fingernails down his back, murmuring, "Bash, that was incredible."

He rained kisses across her face and eyelids and then gave her a smirk. "I thought for a second, you were gonna crush my skull with your knees."

She narrowed her eyes. "I'm sure you can get out of

the way before you become a fatality."

"Not even gonna try, baby," he rolled back onto the pillows with his arms behind his head, "I'll be one lucky son of a bitch if *that's* how I get to die."

She got up to move the tray to the nightstand, fed him a strawberry, and handed him a glass of wine. "You're not allowed to die."

He took a sip and shamelessly ogled her body as she shimmied out of the gown and into one of his t-shirts. Remembering his conversation with Drew about them having limited time left to enjoy such things, he fought off a pang of premature grief.

Catching the look on his face, she snuggled next to him. "What's the matter?"

"Nothing," he pulled her close, "but I want to remember absolutely everything about this night."

Chapter Five

"You dumb whore!"

Chuck and Bash ran up, guns drawn, on either side of the Schmidt's back porch just as the fight inside escalated. From the window it looked as if Dirk Schmidt was covered in blood.

"Aw, hell." Bash snarled and kicked in the door.

Dirk had come home drunk after his night shift at the mattress factory and when she threw a fit about it, Holly was backhanded and thrown around the room for her trouble. By the time the deputies arrived, she'd had enough and hurled the slow cooker at him. They found both Dirk and Holly on the kitchen floor, covered in what they learned was barbecue chicken, not blood.

Chuck knelt and examined her blooming shiner and asked, "You gonna let us arrest him, Holly?"

"Get his drunk ass out of here." She spit in Dirk's direction, "If you come back to this house, I'll kill you and these two Barneys will never find your body."

"You heard her threaten to kill me," Dirk wailed, "and she'll do it, too." He wiped at the sauce on his face,

"This shit burns."

Bash pulled the handcuffs from his belt, kicked Dirk onto his face and waved a finger at Holly. "Woman, you need to shut your mouth." Since she'd said it in front of them, he had to hope she didn't kill Dirk and that was contrary to what he believed to be the best thing for everyone involved.

Bash leaned against the truck after they wrestled him into the back, telling Chuck, "I can't believe he's still drunk."

Dirk was anxious and fidgety on the way to the jail. Leaning into the partition, he huffed hot whiskey breath in their ears, whining, "You heard her, Sheriff Ruiz. You heard what she said."

"What I hear right now is a little bitch in my back seat and you're gettin' on my nerves, man."

"I suggest you try to find yourself one of those cheap, all-in-one lawyers from Phoenix." Bash counted on his fingers and turned in his seat to face their prisoner. "I calculate at least one assault charge and probably a divorce, and that's on the heels of last year's DUI. Am I missing anything, Chuck?"

"I'm sure something else will come up." Chuck said, laughing as Dirk slumped against the window, muttering to himself.

The Chuparosa jail was located at the back of the Sheriff's station and consisted of four cells and a vending machine.

"You want your old room," Chuck mocked as they dragged him through the hallway, "or you wanna try some new scenery?"

"I need to see the preacher."

"McClane?"

The Schmidts attended the nondenominational church, but word around town was that Pastor Jim McClane was running low on patience with that family, not that anyone blamed him.

"No, I need to see Pastor Clarke."

Bash slammed him against the wall. "Hypocrite."

Once, after watching the love of his life absorb a demon, Drew Clarke had too much to drink at Isaac's bar and Dirk complained to Bash that it wasn't a good look for the church.

Chuck opened the cell door, and they tossed him inside. "I'll call Drew, and he'll come to see you, but you don't deserve him."

"Good thing their kids were in school and didn't see them fight," Bash flicked a piece of chicken off Chuck's collar, "Jesus."

They pushed through the back door to find Billy Tate at the front desk unpacking a box of electronics. Billy was a seventy-year-old cotton farmer who sold his land in the nineties to the company that built the mattress factory in the next town over. A widower who raised six boys on his own, including two that just showed up over the years, he'd been a fixture in Chuparosa as long as anyone could remember.

Since selling his land, he came and went through town on no particular schedule and didn't answer any questions about it. He took a job at Racine's the last time he was there, helping Molly keep the restaurant afloat after her husband passed away. Chuck hired him more recently to keep an eye on things when he and Bash were out of the office, which was most of the time.

Chuck peered at him. "What are you playing with over there, Billy?"

"Those dipshits at county are all mixed up," he complained, "they didn't send us the horse tack you ordered, but we did get a bunch of high-tech surveillance equipment."

"Crap," Chuck poked through the box, "what are we gonna do with all this?"

Bash laughed and hung his cowboy hat on a hook by his desk. "Some guy in Scottsdale is scratching his head over our new cinches as we speak."

"Oh, and Bash," Billy gestured toward the waiting room, "there's some old geezer here to see you."

"Old compared to who? You?"

"Go on punk," Billy snipped, "and Drew Clarke's on his way—you're welcome."

Bash took a peek through the door and stiffened, recognizing right away who waited there. Chuck took note of the stone-cold look on his friend's face and instinctively rested a hand on his sidearm.

"Bash?"

"I know him."

The visitor stood up slowly and held out his hand, but Bash turned his back on him and said, "Get out."

"Son, you don't understand."

Bash clenched his fists and with a voice full of hatred, said, "What did you call me?"

The old man swallowed hard but stood his ground. "Sebastian, we need to talk."

"I got nothin' to say to you."

"It's important."

"I said get out."

Billy picked up the twelve-gauge shotgun and racked the slide. "Now, look here. Bash is askin' you nice, but I ain't."

"Is everything alright?" Drew pushed through the door and exchanged glances with Chuck.

"Excellent timing, Preacher," Billy said, keeping the shotgun on the stranger, "this guy is doin' his best to meet God."

The man tried to search Bash's eyes, but he turned away again. "That's fine," he said and made his way to the door. "but I'll be back."

"Not today," Billy advised.

Chuck moved his hand from his pistol to Bash's shoulder. "Talk to me, man."

Billy set down the shotgun, poured himself a cup of coffee and returned to his desk. He picked up the phone, and before he dialed said, "Only one man can provoke that kind of reaction from another."

"You're right, Billy." Bash stood frozen in the middle of the room. "That was my father."

Warren Scott left Bash and his mother when Bash was six years old, returning every now and then when he needed money or a place to stay. Warren *borrowed* from his ex-wife more often than he ever helped with expenses, but Lilly Scott was determined that her son get to know his father. On the few occasions she was able to guilt him into spending time with Bash, they were both so miserable that the boy took to running away to get out of it.

Warren wasn't officially a criminal, but he rarely had a permanent address that Bash could remember, and he was always working on some kind of get-rich-quick angle. No matter where he stayed, there were women around all the time and there was never anything to eat. Eventually, Warren stopped answering Lilly's calls and then disappeared altogether, leaving them with no money at all and no inkling of his whereabouts.

The authorities didn't go after dead beat dads back then, but Bash thought they were better off without him anyway. It killed him to see his mother work so hard though. He adored her and considered them a team, contributing to the household funds as soon as he could get a legitimate job, and even a little bit before then. Despite her protests, he insisted on giving her money every month until she died.

"Maybe he just needs cash," Chuck offered.

"I couldn't be that lucky."

"Listen, we're good here, man. Go home. Better yet, go wash your truck and take Laura for a drive. It's supposed to be a beautiful night."

Drew sat on the corner of Bash's desk. "Chuck could be on to something, Bash. He is pretty old. Maybe he just wants to make amends with you before he dies."

"Yeah," Billy hung up the phone," "probably just an old man tryin' to get into Heaven."

Bash watched, unblinking, from the window as his father disappeared down the street. "I hope he goes to Heaven so I never have to see him again."

Billy flipped a new box of twelve-gauge shells open on the desk. "You surely won't be *that* lucky."

Laura filled up a cooler with sandwiches, snacks and beers while waiting for Bash to get home. Dressed for the outdoors in jeans, hiking boots, and one of his flannel shirts, she was waiting at the door.

"What's going on, baby?"

"Billy called."

"Oh, yeah?" He hung up his hat and let her take him

into her arms.

"He said you were planning to take me for a ride."

He bent his head and breathed in her scent. Until the end of his days, he would never smell lavender or vanilla without yearning for her touch.

"What else did that old coot tell you?"

She didn't bother to demure. "He said that Warren showed up at the station today."

He tensed at the mention of his father's name, so she kissed lightly along his jawline. He closed his eyes, relishing her affection, but he would not allow himself to relax.

"Why would he come for me?" he wondered aloud, "Why now?"

"We'll talk about it tonight," she assured him, "and we'll figure it out."

Watson followed him around, worried for his *big man* as he changed his clothes and loaded the cooler into the truck.

"I'm okay, boy."

Bash waved him into the back seat and gave Laura his hand as she stepped up. Chuparosa had dozens of dirt roads that lead nowhere in particular, and he took their favorite one. Bash was lost in thought on the drive, so Laura used the time to reflect on what she knew about his childhood.

She'd met his mother on a few occasions, but Lilly died only a couple of months after they started dating. Laura liked her very much, though privately she questioned her decision to try forcing a relationship between Bash and her ex-husband.

Life for a single mother in the two thousands was hard enough and she couldn't imagine how Lilly must have struggled in the eighties without the privilege of being able to rely on a sister and close friends for moral support. Lilly fought, often unsuccessfully, to keep Bash out of trouble, having no small-town village like Laura's to help her, and she worried constantly for her willful son.

Laura never tried to do that herself and was grateful that Brian's dad stayed away after he abandoned them. From the beginning, she truthfully answered all of Brian's questions and allowed him to draw his own conclusions. The reality was that since she'd painted no real picture of the man, Brian used his imagination to create a version of his father so monstrous that he was almost afraid to think of him.

Horrified when she'd learned of this, she asked Brian if it wouldn't have been easier to imagine him as some kind of faraway hero, but Brian said heroes take care of their children, they don't leave them. As far as she knew, they never sought each other out, but she always wondered if some part of Brian might resent her for not trying harder to build him a more traditional family.

Laura just didn't see the point in begging a man who didn't want her or their child to stick around. It was difficult to say if one mother's philosophy was any better than the other's and she wished they could have compared notes, but there wasn't enough time.

On the other hand, she had nothing to say to Warren Scott and was incensed by his audacity. Something prickled in the back of her mind though, warning that whatever he wanted was somehow a piece of the same deadly puzzle that they'd been working on for months.

Bash parked the truck near a towering black rock covered in petroglyphs that had been split in half probably centuries before. Though they never dared, there was space enough to walk between the two giant pieces. As a precaution, Laura sprinkled sugar cubes around assuming it was a portal to, at best, the Other Side. At worst, who knew? Despite the potential for danger, the aura surrounding the place was soothing and they often climbed to the top of the rock fragments to relax and absorb the energy.

At sunset, Bash dropped the tailgate and helped her arrange their dinner, he and Watson noting cheerfully that she included some of the peanut butter cookies that were baked that morning. Belly full and beer in hand, Bash laid his head in her lap and stared up at the stars.

"It's going to be one hell of a week. He's out there, just waiting for the right time to ambush me again."

She ran her fingers through his hair, choosing her next words carefully. "You know you can take control of the situation if you find him first and make him tell you what he wants."

"Don't you see?" He sat up, shaking his head in frustration, "I don't care what he wants."

"He won't stop. Wouldn't you rather deal with him on your own terms?"

"I'm not going to deal with him at all. Those *are* my terms and he's just gonna have to accept it."

She disagreed, knowing it would never be that simple, but it wasn't her decision to make, and she could certainly understand where Bash was coming from. "No matter what," she touched his cheek, "I'm on your side."

He laid back down and became quiet again. He

knew she thought he was wrong but loved her fiercely for standing by him anyway. His breathing slowed as he focused on the clear night sky and the sounds of the desert. Millions of insects chirped incessantly, and a mockingbird sang out from a mesquite tree. Every now and then the coyotes would yip to each other, but all the surrounding activity only enhanced a sense of stillness in them that they treasured. Until, from a distance there came a long, loud howl.

Bash sat up and pulled Laura into a protective embrace. "Christ, what now?" he muttered.

Watson paced, looking from his parents to the darkness but after listening hard for a few minutes, there was nothing else. They were hesitant to return to the real world, but Watson nudged at their knees, urging them to leave.

Bash noticed then that the desert had gone silent and took her hand. "I think it's time to go."

The howling started again, and it was much closer. He picked her up and dashed around to the driver's side of the truck, hearing whatever it was running toward them in the sand.

He flung open the door and shouted, "Watson! Now!"

Their dog jumped in and snapped his jaws on Laura's shirt, tugging on her while Bash pushed her inside. He climbed in after she scrambled over the center console and slammed the door shut just as the thing ploughed into the truck, rocking it with the force of its body. Laura jammed on the lock button while Bash scanned the area and fumbled with his keys.

"I can't see it!"

She pressed her face to the window and screamed,

"It's on this side!"

He started the engine and gulped when the lights came on. It was a man, hunched over, hairy and grotesque, his face twisted and enraged, with claws scratching the ground as he prepared to run at them again.

He put the truck in gear, and the hunched man hit the passenger side, dragging its claws across the door and then smashing its head through the window. It was as if the door exploded with glass shattering into the truck. The creature grabbed Laura by the arm and tried to drag her through the broken window.

Bash held her by the waist and Watson lunged, snapping his jaws until the thing released her and she screamed again, "Go, Bash, go!"

He floored the engine, and the strange creature ran along side of them for several minutes before they left him behind, and though he disappeared from the review mirror, his infuriated howling followed them for miles.

They burst through the door at home, locking it behind them and peering out the windows.

"I don't think it followed us," Laura gasped.

Bash pulled them into the light, examining her and Watson for injuries.

She had never seen anything like him, but there was something familiar to her about the tortured looking man and she couldn't put her finger on it until later that night. While watching him get ready for bed, she realized what it was. The monster that tried to kill them in the desert had Sebastian's eyes.

Chapter Six

"You're thinkin' too hard Bash, you're gonna hurt yourself."

Billy and Drew were finalizing the logistics of transferring Dirk Schmidt to a rehabilitation center in Prescott while Bash sat at his desk, tapping a pencil on his chin. He'd been lost in thought about the night before and barely heard a word they were saying.

"You *are* a million miles away this morning," Drew agreed.

Bash made a face and left his seat for a cup of coffee. "Hey, Chuck offered me his cabin in Pinetop this month. Do you and Sarah want to go with us?"

Chuck stormed in before Drew could answer.

"Bash! Jesus Christ, are you okay?"

Bash looked down at himself, "I think so."

"Laura's on the phone with Mena right now going on about how you two barely got away from some kind of monster last night. She says you saved her life."

Drew and Billy shared a look and moved in closer.

Bash chuckled, "She's braggin' on me?"

Billy rubbed his temples. "Preacher, can your God save me from this idiot of a man?"

Drew gave Billy's arm a sympathetic squeeze and waved his hand to get Bash's attention. "So, you did go for a drive? What happened?" He then interrupted as Bash relayed the story. "You didn't think to tell us about it first thing this morning?"

Bash shrugged. "I'm still trying to figure out what it was."

"Laura told Mena you were flying across the desert like Thelma and Louise."

"You were Louise in that scenario, right?"

Bash ignored Billy and led them outside to inspect the broken window and the dents in his truck.

"Laura saged the shit out of this thing last night, and I'm gonna see what Arley's guys can do with the mess."

Bash had said it was scratched, but Drew rubbed his hand across what he considered to be deep gashes in the doors. "A werewolf maybe?" He shuddered, thinking about how close his friends had been to those claws. *If a werewolf had scratched Laura...*

"No, it was human—wearing clothes and everything, but the way he looked...it was just...it was just wrong."

"It was your brother, Sebastian."

The men gathered around Bash as Warren Scott stepped around the truck.

Bash winced. "You're a liar."

"His mother found me a few days before she died and said Nick had been acting strange and that she was afraid."

"Nick? His mother?" Bash leaned against the truck and put his hands on his knees. "Don't. Don't you put this on me. I don't want to hear anymore."

"It was years ago," Warren persisted, "but things didn't work out with me and Gloria. When Nick came along, I couldn't...well you know I'm just not a family man. But she was so upset when she called, I figured I ought to do something, so I followed him for a few days. I swear to you he's made a deal with some kind of devil—I saw it myself, but I think it cursed him and turned him into that awful thing. Then Gloria died and I didn't know what to do so I tracked you down, thinking that you could stop him."

"Stop him from what?" Chuck asked.

Bash looked up. "How did Gloria die?"

"It was heart failure. I think he scared his poor mother to death." Believing he'd finally piqued their interest, Warren's speech got bolder. "Listen here, Sebastian, a long time ago, I accepted that things will never be right between me and my boys, but you have to help your brother."

"Your boys? How many are there?" Bash advanced on him. "If I'd known I had even one brother, this might never—"

"Warren," Drew stepped between them, "how old is Nick?"

"Let's see..."

"He has no idea." Bash was disgusted, and his eyes took on a wild, faraway look as he tried to process the fact that everything he thought he knew about his father was turning out to be much worse. He assumed when Warren left his family that all the damage was done and, with varying degrees of success, Bash had spent his life making peace with the pain.

It seemed though that because his father apparently

scattered heartbreak wherever he went, Bash would probably never know the true extent of the suffering gathered under the Scott name. In that way, Warren had cursed all of his offspring, and they might never even get to know each other. Growing up, and even as an adult, he'd always wanted a brother. He hadn't thought it possible to feel any more bitterness toward Warren, but there it was. He'd robbed him of a father and a sibling.

"You said you saw it," Drew started, "what is it that you think cursed him?"

"Aw, maybe the kid just ate too much paste in kindergarten and it's finally catching up with him." Billy sniffed.

"I don't know what it was, but I know it had horns, like the Devil."

The other men heaved a collective sigh. They were familiar with any number of things that had horns and none of them as friendly as the Devil.

"Leave me alone." All of a sudden, Bash was bone tired and he walked away, telling Warren, "I'm going on vacation."

"Is this you trying to get revenge on me?" Warren called after him. "Is that what this is? Ignore me all you want to, son, but you can't ignore him. He's out there and he's coming. He's coming for you!"

They found Bash at the stables and paused near the door to assess their friend's mental state. Not one of those men could be called stoic, least of all Bash, but he'd put a saddle on Tess, and they relaxed a bit, watching him chat with her lovingly as he brushed her mane.

Together, they'd gone through any number of horrors but each of them found it easier to heal from the wounds inflicted by actual monsters than the ones left behind by their parents.

There was no limit to what Drew would have given to raise even one child of his own and he was still twitching with outrage over the way Warren had so flippantly dismissed his responsibilities.

"Chuck, tell me how a grown ass man can walk away from two families," he held up his fingers, "two little boys."

"That we know of."

Drew let his head fall backward and looked at the sky. "It's not that comforting but Daniel would say it's just fate, and probably has more to do with Warren's fate than his sons'."

"Nah, man," Chuck kicked at a clod of mud dried onto the door frame. "That's an unacceptable reason for the way Bash feels right now. Fate is bullshit."

They saddled up as well and Bash led them to where he and Laura had been attacked the night before.

"Hear that?" He and Chuck dismounted and drew their guns. "Nothing. No insects, no birds—nothing."

There were deep scratches in the dirt, and they could see where Bash had spun his tires to get away. The mockingbird lay dead on the ground near the mesquite tree it had been perched in.

Drew and his horse, Stranger, followed Nick's tracks to the split rock. "Look at this."

Slashes marred the stone and there were bloody handprints with clumps of hair smeared across some of the petroglyphs.

"Was he on the Other Side?"

Drew reached out to one of the petroglyphs and it warmed under his touch, emanating a soft glow. He turned in the saddle and said, "Hey, did you know they did this?"

Then, Adira stepped through the split in the stone, startling Stranger who reared up and tossed Drew flat on his back with a heavy thud.

Chuck kicked away a sharp rock Drew had miraculously missed with the back of his head and Bash crouched beside him to assess the damage. Drew groaned pitifully and rolled onto his side, the pain radiating from his spine to his fingertips and down his legs.

"Take it easy, man."

They helped him to his knees while he caught his breath.

"Anything broken?"

He did a few neck rolls and moved his arms back and forth. "I don't think so."

Bash was doubtful, picking stickers off the back of Drew's dusty shirt. "I wonder if we could hire Noah full time. Just for us."

Drew glared at Stranger and grumbled, "We had a deal."

The horse lowered his head and dragged a hoof through the sand as if he felt bad, but he and the other horses nervously kept their eyes on the mountain lion. Adira waited patiently while the men assured each other that Drew would be alright.

The Deane sisters had trained them to carry sugar cubes in their pockets in case they ever needed an offering, so when the Bobs popped their heads through the portal behind Adira, Drew was ready.

"Treats?"

"Treats?"

He rubbed at his back and leaned against the split stone, holding out a handful of sugar. The bobcats lapped up all his cubes and took their places flanking Adira. At last, the men heard her voice in their heads.

"When Laura killed the troll, her message was acknowledged on the Other Side by all but the one they call Jaya.

"Is that who attacked us last night?"

"Jaya has hidden deep within the Other Side for thousands of years, waiting and plotting. Most of us believe that she is the only one of her kind and...that she is insane."

"Fabulous," said Chuck, rubbing the bridge of his nose.

Adira looked around and flicked her ears in annoyance. "Pay attention to what I say: Nicholas was following Jaya's instructions, and it was *he* who attacked you. She has creatures from another realm at her disposal—I have never seen their kind before. They cannot cross over to the Other Side, but they lured him here...to her."

"To get to me...to get to Laura." Bash put his head in his hands.

Adira nodded. "Jaya has become obsessed with the angel witches and Nicholas has bargained deeply with her. What he has done goes beyond blood magic or any of the spells that foolish troll took on himself."

Bash straightened his back. "We'll have to go to the Other Side to stop them."

"Nicholas cannot return to the Other Side until his

half of the bargain is completed."

Drew glanced at the blood on the split rock. "He was trying pretty hard to get back in last night." Afraid he already knew the answer, he took an uneasy breath and asked, "What is the other realm you spoke of Adira?"

She swished her tail and turned to leave. "When I first met Thomas, he referred to it as Hell."

"What in the world have you been into Bash?" Arley Davis opened the driver's side door of Bash's truck and scratched his head.

"You think you can pound this out, Beau?"

Arley had owned Chuparosa Gas and Service pretty much since Chuparosa came into existence and he was always in the shop, even though he'd recently retired and handed the business over to his son, Beau.

"The window won't be a problem and I can pull this dent out," Beau said, "but I'll have to order some parts for the passenger side. This Tundra is what they call midnight black, right?"

Bash ran a hand through his hair, exceedingly grateful for their nonjudgmental assessment of the situation. "I appreciate it."

Drew leaned against a stack of tires while Bash uncomfortably explained the cause of the damage. He'd followed in his 4Runner to give Bash a ride home and, hopefully, get him to talk a little bit. Sarah said that Laura was worried about him, and she wasn't the only one.

A fair amount of Bash's personal problems were self-inflicted, but though he tended to take the long way around, he would eventually sort himself out. Even so, no one could have been prepared for the kind of bombshell Warren dropped on him.

Bash knew his stubborn attempts at ignoring his father would continue to backfire, but the only man he could truly say he hated had foisted this fresh horror on him and he was going to indulge himself like any neglected child would.

However unpleasant, Adira had given them some good leads, and Drew knew Bash would feel more in control if he could start treating it like any other investigation.

"You know," Beau continued, "the kids were telling me they seen somethin' scratching around near the Devil's Mouth the other day."

Bash raised an eyebrow and Drew smiled to himself as his friend's demeanor shifted into the confident sheriff mode that the Davis's were more accustomed to. He asked Beau if he could drop by later and talk to the kids about what they saw.

"Whatever we can do to help," Beau said, "I feel bad now because I thought they were full of shit, and Genie's gonna kill 'em when she finds out they were playing around that abandoned mine."

"Tell them to stay away from there," Bash warned. Then he smiled, "Say Arley, I thought you were retired. Shouldn't you be out fishing or something?"

Beau sniffed, "He'd rather hang around here and be a nuisance to me."

"I wanna make sure he don't lose any of our customers."

"Where else they gonna go, Dad?"

"It's the urban sprawl," Arley told them, "soon

there'll be service stations on every corner."

"Built into the mountains that are currently on every corner, I suppose." Beau chuckled.

"Besides," Drew was doubtful, "do you really think Chuparosa would let that happen to itself?"

They looked around uneasily until Arley admitted, "I guess the Preacher's got a point, but you never know."

Drew drove the long way when they left Arley's place, hoping Bash would open up a little bit about his father. He wasn't in the mood to talk about his family, but didn't seem to mind the drive, folding his arms and resting the back of his head against the seat. Bash hadn't been sleeping well even before Warren came to town, and the exhaustion was becoming a heavy load. His eyelids drifted downward and within seconds, more of the horrible images he dreaded came to life in his mind.

From the window he saw Stranger rear up and Drew disappear into the bushes. Turning in his seat, Bash realized he was alone in the 4Runner and pushed open the door. He met Chuck on his way to where Drew had fallen, and they ran for what seemed like miles before coming upon the opening of a mine shaft.

They climbed down and called out to him but heard nothing until a woman's scream echoed through the tunnel.

Drew was nowhere in sight when they reached the bottom, but Sarah lay unconscious against the wall. As they ran for her, the creature Bash had learned was his brother shoved an ore car in their path, knocking them off their feet. Nick moved toward Sarah as she began to stir and when they tried to stop him, their bodies sank into the sand. They held tight to the ore car, but the pull of the sand was too much, and the last thing Bash saw before it covered his head was Nick grabbing Sarah by the hair.

He sat up bolt right, catching his breath while Drew explained that for a full five minutes, he'd been trying to shake him out of a nightmare. Bash pulled out his phone but was shaking too badly to dial. "Call Sarah. Now."

Drew did as he was told and then reported that both Sarah and Laura were hiking with Watson and that they were fine.

Bash tapped his fist on the dash. "Jesus, that's getting embarrassing."

"Embarrassing?" Drew chuckled. "You had to give me a drunken shower once so I'm afraid I win that game. Forever."

Looking into Drew's worried eyes, Bash took a breath and added, "I know you want to ask about it so go ahead."

He let Bash collect his thoughts for a minute and then tried to ask as few questions as possible while getting the most information out of his agitated friend.

"How often does it happen? Are they always the same?"

"I've had nightmares my whole life," Bash said. He looked out the window, almost surprised to see the people on the street behaving normally. "But they've never been so violent, or so real."

Drew remembered Samuel's appalling vampire story. "Is it Adam?"

"When Adam's there, he's in trouble and in pain,

just like the rest of us."

"Is it worse since the Tromluí?"

Bash nodded and then neither one of them said anything else for the rest of the drive. After dropping him off, Drew turned down a dirt road and pulled over to think. He lowered all the windows to let in the fresh air and though it wasn't what Midwesterners would call a crisp fall day, it was cool enough outside that the breeze against his skin gave him goosebumps.

When he prayed in those days, especially after meeting the angels, the heartbreakingly one-sided nature of the conversations became almost too much for him to bear. After begging for his life that day in the baptismal, his attempts over the years at cultivating a divine relationship had left an empty hole inside of him. Fearing that hole would fill with resentment, he finally chose to focus his prayers on those he cared about and abandoned any hope of a connection deeper than that.

Bash had so many rough edges that they rubbed inward against his veins and a fair amount of the good he did was accidental, but he was the most loyal man Drew had ever known. He would follow someone he loved into Hell and very nearly did once. So, resting his forehead on the steering wheel, Drew whispered a simple, heartfelt request that Sebastian be freed from his nightmares, if only for a little while.

As he raised his head, a gray kit fox with a ring of black fur around its front left paw peeked around a barrel cactus and blinked at him. He'd seen that fox when they first met Adira in the canyon, what seemed like a million years ago.

"Hey pal, how've you been?"

Sarah would have said that the fox showed up to

bring him encouragement, but since Drew didn't know that he just thought it was cool.

Chapter Seven

"Look over here!"

Torrential downpours during the summer monsoon season often sent flash floodwaters plunging off the canyon ledges. They flowed over the white granite rocks that jutted out from the mountain sides and up from the riverbed creating impressive, if temporary, waterfalls throughout the area. It was October though, and it hadn't rained in weeks so when Laura found herself ankle deep in a puddle of mud, she turned in nervous circles looking for the source of the rushing water.

She and her sister hiked deep in the mountains with Watson that day to gather the necessary plants for a variety of spells they'd been working on. Sarah hastily tucked a small handful of purple flowers in a pouch on her waist, careful to remove her rubber gloves and zip it all together before trotting off in the direction of Laura's voice.

A nasty rash from a spell ingredient was a rookie mistake neither of them had made since they were teenagers, and she wasn't about to let those flowers touch her skin. Poisonous as it was, scorpion weed could help a person face their fears and come to grips with any unfortunate mistakes that may be haunting them.

A person like Nicholas Scott. Bash didn't want to hurt his brother, but Laura didn't want him to hurt Bash, so she'd crafted a dangerous, but powerful spell to bind him to them so he couldn't do any harm away from Chuparosa. She'd made another one to, if necessary, banish him forever.

Watson charged ahead and then waited patiently while Sarah followed Laura up the side of the cliff, stopping short in amazement when they reached the ledge. A waterfall poured over the mountaintop and into the canyon, splashing heavy droplets down to where they'd been foraging for plants below.

"That explains all the puddles." Laura stuck out her hand and let the water flow through her fingers, noting that the sand under their feet sparkled like crystals in the sunlight. In her peripheral vision, the desert tilted slightly to the left and the bushes seemed to grow fuller around her. Her eyes fluttered closed while her mind adjusted to the unsteady sensation.

"We must be on the outskirts of the Other Side."

"Drink."

"Drink."

The Bobs emerged from a cave behind the fall and stuck their tongues in the spray as if it were a water fountain.

"We probably shouldn't do that," Sarah warned, "but this is as good a place as any to stop for lunch."

"Lunch?"

"Lunch?"

The Bobs eyed Watson cautiously, but he busied himself with a bowl of turkey and cheddar chunks that Laura placed in front of him. So, they hovered with no shame waiting for the women to find a dry spot on the cliffside to unpack their sandwiches.

In the regional park area, there was what the county almost jokingly referred to as a waterfall about a mile into the most touristy of the mountain trails. It was supposedly the only active waterfall that remained after the canyons were formed, certainly since the climate began to change and Arizona entered its long-lasting drought. There was never more than a trickle of water into a small green pool at the base of some damp, slimy rocks, and the residents of Chuparosa never went there.

The gushing waterfall in front of them though was nothing short of spectacular. They texted Bash and Drew a few pictures and pinged their location. If it was on the Other Side, they might never find it again, but even if they couldn't bring their lovers someday, they intended to enjoy it themselves for as long as they could.

Sarah popped open a can of sparkling water and asked, "What do you want for your birthday?"

Laura had thus far been able to avoid any discussion of her fiftieth birthday, but since it was rapidly approaching, she sighed inwardly and started the mental gymnastics necessary to accept the half-century notch in her timeline.

"I'm getting a tattoo."

She'd always wanted one but could never before commit to a design or a bodily location.

"I'll get one to match then," Sarah announced. Rueben would have freaked out if she'd gotten a tattoo, and she was at once fired up about the idea.

"What do you want?"

"I don't care, it's your birthday."

Laura was relieved that Sarah had no preference because she'd thought about it for months. Bash had a compass on his chest, there was an owl on Drew's shoulder made up of Celtic knots, and Audi had recently gotten a pair of miniature angel wings inked onto her upper back. After years of dithering, it was so obvious as she looked out over the red flowering bushes dotting the desert around her. Her beloved town was named after the favorite flower of her favorite animal.

"How about matching hummingbirds on our wrists?"

"How about hummingbirds with halos?" Sarah countered.

"Perfect."

"When you speak of your birthday, do you mean the *anniversary* of the day you were born?"

Adira leapt from above, startling them and setting the Bobs, who'd been lounging in the shade nearby, to attention. "Is it a holy day for humans?"

"Not necessarily holy," Laura gave each bobcat a piece of turkey from her sandwich, "but I'm going to be fifty years old and that's a pretty big deal—especially for women because we go through so many physical and cultural changes during this time of our lives."

"You hit the age of invisibility when you can't have children anymore," Sarah said flatly. "No one likes to think about us old hags."

"But you are only a child," Adira flicked her ears, "without even a century to your credit, and you've not even fully learned your craft."

Laura didn't feel like a child, but she didn't feel like

an old hag either. It was true that her skin had some wrinkles and that there were thin streaks of white in her hair, but like her sister, she resented the implication that the number fifty somehow took away from the fact that she was still an active, healthy, sexual, and productive human being.

The big cat stretched long, indicating her comfort level with the women but, lest there be any confusion over status, returned immediately to her standard regally seated position. "What you do with this time now is what you'll be remembered for."

Sarah wasn't sure she completely agreed, but Adira's words emphasized an emptiness she'd been feeling.

"My whole life revolved around my family and my job, and I guess I kind of lost myself somewhere along the way. Now, I don't know what I want to do."

She was dying to know the mountain lion's age, but instead asked if she had a husband or children of her own.

"I have yet to encounter a worthy male," she said.

The sisters looked at each other and convulsed with laughter.

"Adira," Laura sputtered, "I could have saved myself so much trouble over the years with that mindset."

Adira tossed her head. "Humans could save themselves all manner of trouble with a different mindset." She issued a low growl at the Bobs who had been sneaking nibbles from the remains of Laura's sandwich and the three of them disappeared behind the waterfall.

"Well, she's not wrong," Sarah sniffed and began packing up her things.

"I don't want to leave just yet." Laura closed her eyes and let the roar of the waterfall engulf her senses while focusing on some of the ones she loved. Next to her, a surge of unexpected joy passed through Sarah, and up north Brian's sour mood lightened.

She hesitated when her intention settled on Bash. Failing to cure his nightmares weighed heavily on her but she hoped he knew she would never stop trying, and that her love for him would never stop growing.

They spotted a group of fairy duster bushes on the way down and gathered some of the delicate pink flowers. The powder puff like blooms would help ground them during their spell work and diffuse the mental instability that was likely to come with such intense magic.

When everything was packed in the Jeep, Sarah offered to drive. "You seem a little off."

"Just stretched kind of thin this afternoon," Laura smiled and accepted the offer.

Assuming Laura was suffering from something hormonal, Sarah grumbled, "Perimenopause is such a bitch. You would make millions if you developed a tea for that."

Laura laughed and said, "If I could figure that out, I would give it away for free."

At home, Bash paced the house, still aggravated by his nightmare in front of Drew. The dreams were worse than ever and it was looking like he would never be able to rest again. Just as panic threatened to engulf him, a serene sensation of strength and belonging wound its way through his anxious mind, and his waning confidence soared. Filled with energy, he went out for a walk, wishing he could share the moment with Laura.

Thinking of her, he stopped short in the driveway and pressed a hand to his chest. His eyes reddened as he realized that it was her supportive presence he'd sensed in the house and though she wasn't there physically, he could feel Laura in his heart.

* * *

Holly Schmidt stumbled out the door of Isaac's Oasis that night and fell in between Drew and Sarah as they walked in. It was well known that Dirk's wife found his alcoholism revolting, so she wasn't much of a drinker herself, but word around town was that she'd been experimenting quite a bit since he went away. Drew and Sarah didn't recognize the man Holly was with, but he wore expensive clothes and an uncomfortable look on his face. Sarah worried, wondering just how far beyond beverages Holly's experimentation had gone.

When Holly noticed them holding hands, she clucked her tongue. "Pastor Clarke, I heard your attendance numbers are going down fast—not that they were ever that large." Though her words were slurred, there was no doubt that everyone in the bar could hear her. "You ought to be more careful about who you run around with. The Deanes are probably hexing your church behind your back."

Sarah had dealt with comments like that her entire life and, for his protection, instinctively tried to put some distance between herself and Drew but he wouldn't let go of her hand. Instead, he gave Holly a grim smile and matched her in volume.

"I count on good people like you to put those rumors to rest. By the way, have you heard from your husband? Is he all settled in up north?"

Holly's cheeks burned, and she pursed her lips, giving her date an expectant look. He and Drew were of a similar age and build but the expensively dressed man wasn't entirely sure what the exchange was all about. As they sized each other up, it was clear that Drew was more invested so Holly's new guy simply took her by the arm and shuffled her outside.

"That may be the most chivalrous thing a man's ever done for me." Sarah gave Drew's hand a squeeze and slipped into the closest booth.

Drew thought the bar was pretty low but kept that to himself. He took a minute as his anger with Holly and compassion for Sarah battled for attention in his heart. Sarah took her own minute and kept her head down, studying the drink menu as if it had changed at all over the last twenty years. She could not imagine living in a place where no one knew or cared about her and would never have the heart to leave Chuparosa. Still, there were times when she would have cheerfully welcomed the coldness of anonymity.

Without looking up, she said, "We used to be friends, but Holly has hated us since high school. She loved Dirk's brother first, but he wouldn't give her the time of day, so she asked Laura for a love spell."

"You're kidding."

Her eyes met Drew's and she added, "You know we don't do that kind of thing, right?" She shuddered, remembering the hateful spells and hexes she'd found in her mother's book of magic. "Anyway, Holly was furious and cornered Laura at a church lock-in—I think they were juniors at the time."

"You just dug up some memories for me," he chuckled, "our lock-ins were absolutely unhinged."

The practice of locking teenagers in the church on a Saturday night was intended to provide them with wholesome social interaction that kept them out of trouble. However, it was Drew's experience that there were as many fights and as much sexual activity at a lock-in as there were in a coming-of-age movie. His youth leaders had only just graduated high school themselves and had their own problems, so supervision was always sketchy at best.

"Well," Sarah continued, "Holly and her sisters ganged up on us and jumped Laura in the foyer. I used my powers and ended up making a big mess of the room. On top of that, Holly sprained her wrist in the fight, so we got kicked out of the youth group," she rolled her eyes, "for promoting devil worship."

"Anyway, after graduation, she found someone in Phoenix to work the spell and then, sure enough, Dirk's brother fell in love with her. They were inseparable."

"But it wasn't what he really wanted. Was it?"

"Gold star for you." Sarah laced her fingers through his, "Messing with free will is tricky business. He died in a dove hunting accident right after they got married. Now, that could have been a coincidence, but more likely, Holly didn't understand the terms of the deal she made. Either way, she convinced herself that she would have lived happily ever after if Laura had just done the spell in the first place and blamed us for his death."

"Dirk weaseled his way into her bed a few months later and well, you know the rest. Our wards have included protection against the Schmidts ever since."

Isaac came by with a couple of beers and sat next to Sarah. "On the house. Holly was in here acting up for hours."

Drew felt bad for Holly, but not bad enough to care that she was gone. He didn't want to talk about the Schmidts anymore and looked around the bar, noticing their friends, Adam and Cara, deep in a heated conversation at a table nearby. They must have been arguing quietly for some time, but Cara was always hyperaware of her surroundings and caught Drew staring. She gave him a fake smile, gripping Adam's arm to let him know that they were on display. Adam's smile was more genuine. He took Cara's hand and led her across the bar, grateful for a break in the tension.

"This is perfect timing!" Cara scooted in next to Drew and leaned across the table. "Shall we discuss Miss Laura's birthday party?"

Weeks earlier, and to an overwhelmingly positive response, she'd floated the idea of a big party for Laura and they'd already arranged to use Isaac's place for the eighties themed event. Isaac hired a Gen-X DJ and was closely supervising the creation of the playlist.

Mena was in charge of decorations and Chuck had been half-heartedly complaining about a New Wave home invasion since she'd unpacked life-sized cardboard cutouts of Duran Duran.

The impromptu meeting turned out to be quite productive as they decided on food, party favors and costumes. Adam was unconvinced of their necessity until Drew confessed that he wouldn't have to look farther than the back of his closet to dress up as a metalhead.

"The *back* of your closet?" Sarah teased. He'd worn

a faded Ozzy Osborne concert t-shirt the day before to the gym. She laughed and confessed, "I wanted to be a Solid Gold dancer when I was fifteen, so I shouldn't make fun."

"I'm not gonna lie," he whispered in her ear, "that's a mental image that will show up in my daydreams for the rest of my life."

The group hushed when Cara mentioned the guest list. Sarah had intended to invite the whole town, but her run-in with Holly was giving her second thoughts about that.

"Good point," Cara agreed, "but then the biggest talk will be about who didn't get invited...and why."

"Ugh," Sarah groaned.

"Besides, your biggest problem will be keeping this thing a secret anyway."

It would be a miracle if Laura was surprised, but Sebastian's only role in the entire production was to police that information and somehow get her into costume and out the door by the appointed hour.

Isaac returned to the bar and the ladies went to the bathroom, so Adam took the opportunity to speak with Drew privately. Word of Warren's appearance had gotten around, and he was concerned about Bash.

"I can't imagine what he's going through. I have to say that I loved my father. He taught me everything about being a man." He looked at his hands as if they were tattooed with the word 'vampire.' "I'm glad he died before he could see me like this."

Drew sat back in the booth and sighed. "I haven't seen mine in years. I'm trying to imagine what I would do if he just showed up, but I also can't imagine a scenario in which he would."

"What about your mother?"

"She thinks what he tells her to think because that's what she was taught to do."

The ladies returned to the table and after some speculation over the nature of Nick's strange affliction, the vampires left for the night and Drew finally had Sarah to himself. He was starving and a little tipsy, making a show of his menu selection.

"It's the same dilemma every time. Cheeseburger or cheeseburger with bacon?" He joked, "Regular fries or curly fries? No one knows how hard it is to be me, Sarah."

She smiled and ran her fingertips along his forearm, sending a pleasant shiver down his spine. He'd been delighted to discover how affectionate she could be and found himself craving her delicate touches when she wasn't around.

As they talked, her thoughts returned to Holly Schmidt and she asked, "Did you know how difficult it was going to be when you chose to get involved with me?"

Since they became a couple, he would have used words like devoted, exhilarating, and indulgent, but never difficult. He leaned forward to kiss her, hoping everyone in the bar could see them.

"I didn't choose you, Sarah. I was blessed with you."

Chapter Eight

The occasional vampire infestation notwithstanding, Chuck fell in love with the town of Pinetop and after years of renting cabins in the White Mountains for family vacations, he and Mena bought one of their own for their thirtieth anniversary. It was a tiny place, but so near one of the many area lakes that the water lulled them to sleep as it lapped at the shore and it backed up to the thick pines of the Apache-Sitgreaves National Forest.

Mena often joked that since they'd been married so long, the cabin purchase resulted from the fact that they even had a joint mid-life crisis. The truth was that it was a dream come true for them and they were happier the day they signed the papers for the cabin than on their wedding day. It was a celebration of everything they'd accomplished in their marriage and, in a way, a renewal of their vows.

Bash and Laura had been there a dozen times, so Chuck was comfortable asking them to help make it snow ready. The cabin would get plenty of use during the winter, but preparations had to be made and Bash was thrilled to have some work to do that would provide a much-needed diversion from his troubles down in the valley. Chuck arranged for a local company called ButtonTop to keep an eye on the place, and one of the owners had even been staying there temporarily.

Angie Walsh was an author trying to find her way in self-publishing and the Ruiz cabin on the lake turned out to be the perfect quiet place to finish her latest book. She and her business partner, Doug Farmer, started ButtonTop as an additional service provided by his forest management company. Their customers either didn't have the time or the inclination to *button up* their cabins before the winter weather months, so Doug and Angie secured the pipes and the boats, cleared the brush, and whatever else was needed. She wrote whenever she could find the time, but since the unexpected success of ButtonTop, that was becoming a rare event.

Thanks in part to Chuck and his distraction-free cabin, she had, in fact, finished her latest work in progress. So, she went above and beyond after he called to let her know his friends would be coming to stay. They were late, so Angie gave them a head start and put fresh sheets on the beds and clean towels in the bathrooms, lit the fireplace, and ordered them pizza from her favorite local place.

When she heard the group pull in, she closed her laptop and met them in the driveway. Bash was driving the Jeep since Beau still had his truck in the shop and Laura hopped out to greet her.

"You must be Angela. I'm so sorry we're late, the traffic was awful."

"Friends call me Angie," she said, sticking out her hand, "nice to meet you all."

Drew and Sarah emerged from his 4Runner and followed Angie to the front of the cabin.

Watson came racing through the trees followed by Bash who yelled, "Hey, stay out of the water 'till tomorrow!"

The German Shepherd stopped at the edge of the lake and looked back in hopes that Bash was kidding, but his *big man's* arms were full of gear, he was tired from driving half the day and his voice was stern.

"I said tomorrow, Watson."

Watson looked once more at the lake and then ran to inspect the new woman. Angie froze when the enormous dog approached but he nudged her hip with his nose until she relaxed enough to pat him on the head. "Where in the world did you find this guy?"

"We rescued each other." Laura took Watson by the collar and said, "Go help Daddy."

Bash's head snapped up. She'd never called him Daddy before, and his entire body tingled as a new turn-on was unlocked inside of him. Had Laura been able to read his mind, she would have pointed out that it was the most unsurprising thing in the world coming from the mind of the man who obsessed over taking care of everyone, particularly her; but since she couldn't, he happily folded that scenario in with his other fantasies and continued to unload the Jeep.

"Let me show you the new boat house door before it gets too dark," Angie said. A chilly breeze drifted off the water as she led them down the dock.

Sarah pulled her sweater around her. "It's very Camp Crystal Lake," she shuddered, "you don't mind staying out here all alone?"

"Jason will have chosen the wrong house, I'm afraid." They turned to see a blonde-haired man with brown eyes and a scruffy beard loaded down with pizza boxes stomping up the driveway. "She's as fierce a fighter as I've ever seen."

"This is my business partner, Doug Farmer," Angie explained.

Bash studied the newcomer as they followed him and the pizza back to the cabin. He assumed Doug came straight from work because his clothes were grubby, and he was covered head to toe in the powdery red dirt that the area was known for. Doug was soft spoken, though he didn't say much as they walked, and Bash thought for sure he'd seen him wince when Angie said, "business partner." The phrase had taken the wind out of his sails a bit.

"Oh, you outdid yourself, Angie," Laura cooed as they entered the cozy living room, "how can we repay you?"

Angie shook her head. "I don't think I could have finished writing my book if Chuck hadn't let me stay here, so I'm the grateful one."

"You finished your book?" Doug set the pizza on the table and took her hands in his, apparently recovered from the "partner" comment.

"Ange, that's great – I'm so proud of you." He beamed at her, then remembered there were others in the room and became self-conscious, letting go of her hands.

The lights flickered in the kitchen, leaving them with only the glow from the fireplace for a few seconds before they came back on.

"Oh, that reminds me," Angie warned, "I don't know what's wrong with that fixture, but I can tell you it's not the bulbs and it's not a ghost."

It would not have surprised them at all if there were a ghost in the cabin, but since Angie had been there for an entire month, they trusted her to have worked that out.

"I'm an electrician, so I'll take a look," Drew promised.

"There's a hardware store in town," Doug offered, "but let me know if they don't come through for you because I can probably get my hands on whatever you need."

Laura picked a book off the coffee table, then pulled an identical one out of her purse and held them up. "You wrote 'The Werewolf's Lover'?"

Angie nodded proudly.

"What are the odds that I'm reading it right now?"

"Is it book two that you just finished?" Sarah bounced with excitement as it was her copy of book one that Laura was reading.

"The Werewolf's Lover?" Drew reached for one of the books and Bash leaned over his shoulder as he flipped through the pages.

He grimaced and said low, "I told you Laura reads some dark stuff."

"Wait a minute...Doug Farmer..." Sarah touched his arm, "are you Doug *the* farmer? The character in the book?"

He blushed and picked up Angie's suitcase. "Are you about ready to go?"

"As far as I know he's not a real werewolf," Angie winked at him, "but he was my inspiration when we became friends."

Bash noticed the slight wince again, but by then he was pretty sure that Doug wasn't uncomfortable being Angie's werewolf muse. He'd winced when she said the word 'friends'. Bash picked up her other bags and walked Doug outside. His truck was standard work white, with clumps of red mud caked on the wheels and splattered up the sides, and the logo for Farmer Forest Management was painted on the doors.

Doug carefully arranged Angie's things in the back seat and then motioned to some trees at the end of the driveway. "See all those cedars?" He scowled as if the trees were guilty of a crime. "That's a fire hazard. Chuck told me I could come by and pull 'em out this week, if it's alright with you."

Bash nodded. "Drew and I would be happy to help, too."

"Didn't you come up here to relax?" Doug snatched an olive-green baseball cap off the dash and put it on, "Fixing electrical and doing yard work doesn't sound like a vacation to me." His cap had a little pine tree embroidered on the front and, like everything else within ten feet of the man, it was covered in red dirt.

"Well," Bash ran a hand through his hair, "this might sound crazy, but that's exactly what we need right now."

Somehow Doug managed to chuckle without smiling and said, "You'd have to try pretty hard to sound crazy to me."

Bash wondered what he meant by that but the crowd from inside spilled into the driveway before he could ask any questions. Doug lurched around to the passenger side and slipped a protective arm around

Angie's waist as he helped her into the truck. Bash had a good feeling about him and looked forward to learning more of his story while they worked together.

As the white truck pulled away, Sarah said, "I know they're business partners, but they would probably make a nice couple."

"Do you think they're already mixing it up a little?" Drew wondered.

Bash lifted an ice chest from the back of the Jeep. "No, but I get the feeling he would very much like to."

Drew's cat, Daphne, was not nearly as outdoorsy as Watson so Audi offered to look in on her while he was up north. As she let herself into his house, a text notification came in from Noah. It had been over a week since their break-up, and he was hoping to talk things out.

She wanted to talk to him more than anything but didn't trust herself not to make things even worse than they already were. Unwilling to cruelly leave him on "read", she didn't open the text, putting off any decisions until she'd had more time to think about it.

Noah's text was all but forgotten though during a frantic ten-minute search, after which she finally found Daphne's orange striped tail poking out from underneath Drew's bed.

"You little diva," Audi bounced on the bed in annoyance, "You knew I was calling your name."

As she hoped, the bouncing was enough of an irritation to rouse the cat, who sprinted into the bathroom and over the side of the tub.

"Oh, no you don't." She scooped her up, noticed

Drew's Scooby Doo hand towels and then eyed Daphne with fresh appreciation. Scanning the room for additional interesting tidbits about her mother's boyfriend, it occurred to her that other than those hand towels, there was nothing much else in the way of decoration.

Drew's theology degree hung slightly askew on the wall next to his Journeyman certification, and there was a picture of him and Sarah on the dresser. The other towels in the bathroom were white along with his sheets and there was a plain gray comforter folded neatly across the foot of the bed. But for the degrees and the picture, it could have been a hotel room.

She closed the bedroom door behind her, tossed Daphne on the floor and picked up a stick with a feather dangling from a string attached to it. They played for a while, but Audi was distracted, unable to get past the lack of home décor. The remote control was on the coffee table next to a pile of open books and an empty mug, so she turned on the television for some background noise as she snooped around.

Despite the state of the little table that he evidently preferred to the desk that collected dust across the room, and about a hundred cat toys strewn about, Drew wasn't a slob. In fact, everything else seemed to be tucked away neatly. Unlike Sheriff Scott, who loved his house and, with her Aunt Laura's help, had turned it into a welcoming home that comforted everyone who entered, it seemed that Drew had never truly settled in to his.

Sitting cross legged on the floor, she rested her palms on Drew's books and tuned into the energy that flowed around the coffee table. He'd been troubled by what he was reading but his innate sense of optimism still hung in the air as if it were left there specifically to offer reassurance to nosy pet sitters. *Stepdaughters? Children?*

Audi jokingly reminded her mother once that she was perfectly happy being an only child, in case she and Drew ever got married, but Sarah had confided in her that he could not have children. So why, as she sat there surrounded by his energy, was the notion of him as a father so strong?

Then she became irrationally annoyed with Sarah, who frequently kept important information from her. She knew that her mother had no intention of having another child though and pushed the intrusive thoughts from her mind, realizing as she did so why Drew's house bothered her so much. The house was just like him—hopeful, but incomplete.

It reminded her of the energy in the house she grew up in, and how unhappy Sarah had been for so many years. Flip-flopping emotionally and finding herself awash in a sudden wave of compassion for her mother, Audi wished for the first time in a while that they could sit and talk the way they used to.

Rather than interrupt everyone's much needed vacation on the lake, she scrolled guiltily past Noah's text and sent one to Sarah wishing her a safe trip that included a picture of the creature from the black lagoon lurching out of the water.

Returning her attention to the coffee table, she frowned while inspecting Drew's books. The titles were disturbing, though she was used to his ever-present Dictionary of Demons. He'd also been studying an odd collection of signs and symbols, protection magic, and the Bible.

Another text came in that she assumed was from Sarah, but she shrieked as Drew's demand lit up her screen: `Proof of life, please.`

She took a short video of Daphne who was batting her empty food dish across the kitchen floor and as her finger hovered over the send arrow a very clear vision of the man appeared before her. They were in her Aunt Laura's old house – her new house. He was outside replacing the hummingbird feeder and Sarah stood nearby giggling while the tiny birds buzzed around his head with impatience. She'd never seen her mother giggle like that and couldn't help but laugh herself.

Through the sliding glass door, she could see that the calendar was on the page for June, and it was the one she bought when the Chihuly exhibit came to her community college. That calendar was for the coming year. It didn't bother her in the least that he would be moving in but there was something that made her uneasy about the circumstances of the move.

A dark mist hovered over the kitchen blurring her sight, and while she was convinced that the vision was mainly cause for celebration, what she couldn't see left a knot in her stomach.

She contemplated this while scooping food into Daphne's dish, but her thoughts were interrupted by the image of her cousin, seconds before the Skyrim theme rang out from her phone. She knew what he wanted to talk about and immediately tried to dissuade him.

"Brian, I'm very busy."

"No, you're not."

"I just had a vision and I'm exhausted."

"Wow, it's been a while."

"Pastor Clarke's gonna move in with us."

"Uh, nice try," he rolled his eyes, "everyone sees that coming."

"Not the way I do."

Her voice quivered in such a way that the hair stood up on his arms. "When's he moving in?"

"Within six months."

"That's good...right?"

"Very," she recalled the dark mist, adding, "I think."

"Before next semester? Are you still planning to take a break from school?"

Though Laura had asked Brian to talk with Audi, the nursing school break was not something that she or Sarah were aware of.

The quiver in her voice deepened into a full sob, "I don't know what I'm doing."

"I do," he gave her a few seconds to catch her breath before going on, "you're panicking. Things are turned upside down for us, but you can't protect everyone, you know. Trust me on that."

"Olivia is safely out of the way."

His heart hardened at the mention of his ex-girlfriend. "It was her choice to make, not mine. I was wrong to hurt her. Besides, Noah was already in on what we do, so don't think for a second that he won't be standing there with the rest of us the next time shit gets real."

"What do you mean, the rest of us?"

"He'll stay away from you, if that's what you really want, but eventually he's gonna move on and it will be us and his new girlfriend...and you." Brian thought back to when he'd seen Olivia outside the gym, sitting on her new boyfriend's lap. "You can trust me on that, too."

Chapter Nine

After Drew and Sarah won the coin toss for the main bedroom, the group began to unpack and settle in. Normally, the witches would use incense to refresh the energy in a new place, but Angie's spark still hung around the cabin, so they decided on simply warding it for protection rather than cleansing away all of her creative passion.

A spritz of Laura's rosemary potion at all the doors and windows, a pentacle wreath out front and cinnamon balls in each bedroom would be enough to keep out most wicked things. For everything else, they had their powers and there were four pistols between them.

The lights in the kitchen flickered off again as Bash and Drew moved food and drinks from the coolers to the refrigerator. Drew retrieved a flashlight from his toolbox, stuck a piece of pizza in his mouth, and left to check the breaker box.

He opened it up and stifled a scream that would have made Sarah's banshee blush as the answer to their problem ran up his arm, jumped from his shoulder and burrowed into a pile of wet pine needles. After regaining his composure, he focused the flashlight and found several loose wires in the electrical panel, each one with tiny bite marks left by the mouse who had been chewing away at the rubber coating before scaring him half to death.

The back door opened, and Bash stepped out carrying two beers and a flashlight of his own. "Find anything?"

Grateful beyond measure that Bash hadn't been there to see him flail in such an unmanly way over the stupid little mouse, he accepted a beer and showed him the damage.

"I doubt the hardware store will have what I need, so we should call Doug tomorrow. In the meantime, I'll tape these up and switch off this breaker. Tell the ladies that it's candlelight only in the kitchen for now."

"Witches forced to use candles...that'll please 'em." Bash chuckled and headed back in the house. "I'm sure there's something in the shed to plug that hole in the box so they don't destroy anything else—I'll be right back."

It was Sarah who brought him the key to the shed. It hung from a piece of hemp twine that she flipped back and forth around her finger. His back straightened as the stars reflected a mischievous gleam in her eyes.

"Looking for this?" She dropped the key in his hand and sashayed toward the shed. The casual dress she wore had been selected as a comfortable road trip outfit, but there was a powder blue ribbon keeping the top together along the scooped neckline that had driven Drew to distraction since they left that morning. The ribbon loosened over the course of the day and after the heavy lifting they'd been doing since they arrived, the loops in the bow had nearly given up under the strain.

Pleased to have her undivided attention, he followed close on her heels, using his flashlight to guide her steps. At the shed, he reached around her to put the key in the padlock, anxious to complete his task and get his fingers in that ribbon. But when the door swung open, she yelped and backed into him so suddenly that he dropped the flashlight. Crouching to pick it up, he realized, as the light shone across the floor of the shed, that she'd been startled by the way it seemed to ripple under the dozens of tarantulas that nested by the door.

He stepped in front of her and raised the flashlight revealing a dusty table saw and a collection of blades that hung from the ceiling with fishing line like ghastly birthday decorations over damp boxes full of rusted wrought iron tools. The air smelled of mold and poison leaching from the chemical bottles that were stacked atop a rotting wooden workbench that leaned dramatically, one leg having been chewed all the way through by...something.

He shivered. "I do not want to know what made those bite marks."

"No wonder Mena calls this Satan's shed. It was like this when they bought the place, and they haven't gotten around to clearing it out." She tugged on his arm, "There's no way we're going in there tonight."

He re-padlocked the door and took her hand, intent on going back to the cabin for another beer and some cuddling in front of the fire.

She tugged on his arm again. "We don't have to go back inside."

The gleam in her eyes reappeared and she walked

him to a section of fence between the shed and the lake. Leaning against a pine tree, she pulled him to her and walked her fingers down his chest, unsnapping the buttons on his shirt along the way.

As he learned how to please her, studying her body's response to every kiss, every touch, and every flick of his tongue, he was continually surprised by what she found exciting. He had never been turned on by danger and he moved the flashlight around, noting that in addition to whatever lurked in the shed, the forest harbored about twenty of its own threats. And those were the ones he could see.

She took the flashlight from him and turned it off, murmuring, "Look at all those stars."

When his eyes adjusted to the darkness, he did not look at the stars but instead focused on her nipples hardening in the chilly breeze. He curled the ribbon around his finger and gave it a tug letting the fabric fall open to reveal that she was not wearing a bra. She buried her hands in his hair as he rained light kisses across the top of her breasts and let his hands travel across her body to learn that she was not wearing anything under the dress at all.

She leaned into him, nibbling at his collar bone as she undid his belt, and his inhibitions fell away. He was so hard for her that he would have done it *in* that creepy shed if she wanted to and was certain he could perform even with all those saw blades hanging over him. Gripping her shoulders, he drove her back against the tree and pushed the front of her dress up her thighs. She pressed her feet into the fence post and rocked her hips to meet him as he slid into her. His languid kisses and the slow deep movement of his hips drove her mad for him.

He was unhurried, enjoying every second of their time together, whispering, "That's my angel," as her breathing quickened.

Angel? She stopped abruptly and took his chin in her hand. "Andrew, did you just call me your angel?"

"I think so," he panicked, "is that okay?"

"I don't know," she pulled him deeper into her, "say it again."

She felt so good that his mind reeled, and he wasn't sure if he could speak at all, but managed, "That's my angel," one more time.

"Yes...yes...again..."

He groaned, "angel..."

Her head fell back against the tree, and she wrapped her legs around him, "Oh, my god, Andrew."

After a while Laura began to worry and sent Bash to the back door window. "Can you see them?"

As the clouds passed across the moon, Bash could see every bit of them and he spun around, snapping the blinds closed.

"Are they alright?"

He made a face. "They're fine."

Laura peeked around him through the blinds and narrowed her eyes. "Good god, they are going to have mosquito bites in the worst places."

"If they're lucky it will only be mosquitos." He shuffled her away from the window and rested his beer against his forehead. "Have you got a spell to make me forget what I just saw?"

"You poor thing." Trying not to laugh, she shook

her head and poured herself a glass of wine. "I'll see what I can come up with to repress memories."

He flopped on the couch in front of the fireplace and pulled her into his arms. "At least he's not dressed like Tarzan."

"What?"

"Never mind."

When the cabin finally quieted for the night, Drew laid in bed on his stomach while Sarah traced around the deep scars on his bare back with her fingers. Years of childhood abuse and neglect had left its mark on all of them, but Drew suffered physically much more than the others.

"Does it still hurt you?" she asked.

"Not on the outside," saying the words, he thought about his scars for the first time in a while, "and not that badly on the inside anymore." He touched her cheek. "I might be unsure of everything about this world, but I'm finally sure about my purpose in it."

Down the hall, Bash got up to use the bathroom, cursing aloud as he stumbled through the pitch black of the cabin. He swore again as he nearly blinded himself by flipping on the light and jumped against the door, spotting his brother Nick hunkered between the sink and the wall.

"What do you want?" he gasped, but Nick only growled in response.

As Nick's long limbs twisted around the pipes, Bash noticed a thick gold ring on his right pinky finger with strange markings engraved in a fiery red stone that was ringed with nuggets of turquoise. The symbol was similar to the one the troll burned into Laura's temple when she was kidnapped.

"What is that? What does it mean?"

Again, Nick said nothing, but he inched away from the sink and began to slink across the floor. Bash reached instinctively for his revolver and of course it wasn't there, but as he looked down, cold water rushed over his bare feet. In the mirror he saw Laura beating on the glass as Richard advanced on her from behind.

"Hey, now," the troll drawled.

Bash knew at once that he had to be dreaming, but there was nothing he could do. He and Nick were held in place by the water freezing around them. In an attempt to free Laura, he lunged his upper body, jerked down the towel rack and threw it at the mirror. It bounced off the glass just as Richard took Laura by the throat.

"No!"

Nick hissed, "The angels did it," and yanked his hand free with that blood curdling howl of his, leaving two fingers behind in the ice, "and now everyone has to pay." He leaned back and pushed off his haunches, leaping at Bash and burying what remained of his claws in his chest.

Bash hollered out and Drew and Sarah raced down the hall as Laura's screams and the crash of the furniture echoed through the cabin. Drew positioned his shoulder, ready to break down their door, but Sarah turned the knob and pushed it open.

The room was in total disarray. Watson paced by the window and Bash leaned against the wall with his head in his hands while Laura rubbed the back of his neck.

She held her hand out to stop them from coming any closer, "We're okay. It was just a nightmare."

Her words were firm, but her fingers were trembling. Drew picked up a glass of ice water and held it close to his eyes for inspection. Bash intended to put it on the nightstand but forgot and left it on the dresser before he went to bed. It had been a couple of hours, but the ice was not melted and Nick's bloody ring floated near the bottom of the glass.

"*Just* a nightmare?"

"Jesus Christ," Bash panted, "Nick was wearing that in my dream." He began to shake uncontrollably.

Laura wrapped her arms around him and said, "Sarah, I left the juniper in the kitchen."

Drew followed Sarah to the other room, dumped the water in the sink and rinsed off the ring. He recalled what Daniel said about the symbol the troll branded Laura with. He'd explained that it wasn't a symbol, but rather part of a language, and specifically a spell. Anger crept into his heart at the thought of Daniel. Where was he? Drew decided then and there to insist on getting contact information from all the angels when they next deigned to show themselves.

Sarah lit a candle and said, "Drew, can you hand me the twine from that drawer, please?" When her request jolted him out of his thoughts, he put the ring in his pocket and did as she asked.

"Walk me though this," he said as she laid out her sister's supplies.

"They've had some success with a similar potion before, but it's just a temporary fix."

She took a small bowl from the cabinet and poured in a fair amount of shea nut oil, then added a few thin cedar chips and a handful of juniper berries.

"The juniper will relax his nerves while the cedar protects him from all of that hostile psychic energy so he can get some deep sleep. I'm sure it's been quite a while."

She dumped the whole mixture into the mortar and pestle and when it was pulverized, she poured it into a jar and gave it a thoughtful shake.

"It's Laura's spell to work, but maybe my two cents will give it a boost."

In her eyes, Sebastian had become the brother she'd never had, and the liquid bubbled to the lid as her love for him flowed through it.

The potion smelled as if they'd ground up a chunk of the forest and Drew leaned over to breathe it in, asking, "Can I help?"

Sarah handed him a spoon and though the bubbles settled down as he stirred, he was quite sure his intentions were clear.

When they returned to the bedroom, Laura was struggling to get compliance out of Bash. "I told you baby, I'll be okay."

He couldn't stand it that he was scaring her, but he didn't know what to do about it. His dreams were no longer an embarrassment, they were a violation, and he was furious. Their bed was sacred space to him where they laughed and made plans and made love and rested safely in each other's arms. That his nightmares were not only invading that space but leaving behind appalling souvenirs was intolerable. He reached for his boots.

"I'm gonna go for a walk."

"Sebastian," she stood between him and the boots, "let me love you the best way I know how."

He sat down hard in the side chair and ran a hand through his hair. "Fine."

Laura took an eye shadow brush from her makeup bag and dipped it in the jar. There was a collective gasp amongst them all when he pulled off his t-shirt, displaying long red welts across his chest. He stared down at the wounds and then up at her, doing his best to keep the hurt out of his voice when he said, "Nick is supposed to be my brother."

Using the potion-soaked brush, she drew a pentacle on his back and another one on his chest. Then she unclasped a thin, silver chain from her wrist and dropped it in the bowl. All of Laura's jewelry had meaning and, on her wrists, she always wore the tiger's eye bracelet Bash bought her in Sedona and the silver chain she bought from her friend Wenona's shop, The Off-World Owl.

The markings on the chain reminded her of the petroglyphs carved in the rocks around Chuparosa and when she mentioned that to Wenona, they talked at length about how the magic on the Other Side probably connected the entire world. The chain was blessed in their friendship but after the spell, it would belong to Bash.

Silver provided added protection for him and as she wove it through the paracord in his shield bracelet, he felt the magic travel from his back, across his chest, and down his arm. His shoulders relaxed and she led him to the bed.

Satisfied that he was no longer a flight risk, Drew

and Sarah backed out of the room and Laura laid down next to him.

He whispered, "I'm sorry, baby," and slept hard for the rest of the night.

It was Drew who ended up outside, alone with his ever-darkening thoughts. He wondered if he was so bad a sinner that he would always be ignored, and he didn't bother to repeat his prayer for Bash.

The night was so black that the moonlight gave the needles on the pine trees the appearance of ice crystals and the lake was so still that if he didn't know any better, he would have thought it a mirage. The forest at nighttime was the perfect metaphor for the state of his faith, but security in the love of his friends and the knowledge that he would kill or die for any one of them without a second thought gave him a sense of peace, even if grace was withheld from above.

Chapter Ten

Drew and Sarah were assigned breakfast on the first morning and it was eerily quiet in the hallway when they woke up, so Sarah put an ear to the other bedroom door. Drew gave her an askant look, but her grin put his mind at ease. She heard only soft laughter as Bash and Laura tried to hush the sounds of their lovemaking.

In the kitchen Drew pulled the eggs and sausage from the refrigerator and said, "That's the only noise that should be coming from their room."

Later, they all sat down for breakfast and planned out their day.

"What are you going to do while we're fishing?" Bash wondered, "we'll be on the lake for hours."

"Oh, you know," Laura batted her eyelashes at him, "probably just mend some socks and miss you."

"That's tomorrow," Sarah corrected, "we're picking berries and churning butter today."

"Oh yeah, sorry...berries and butter. We are on vacation after all."

Bash's lips thinned. "Hilarious."

Laura was grateful for the chance to respond to him with sarcasm rather than the truth. She wouldn't have lied about her plans if he'd pressed, but what they intended to do would make him uncomfortable and she would rather tell him after the fact.

Fueled by sleep, sex, a breakfast burrito, and on his way to go fishing no less, Bash whistled all the way down to the boathouse. Chuck had an aluminum fishing boat with an outboard motor that was large enough to comfortably seat both men and their gear but small enough for the mountain lake. Chuck talked of nothing else for weeks after he bought it and was devastated that he couldn't go with them and take it out again before the freeze.

Careful not to bang his head on the low ceiling of the little house, Drew carefully stepped down to the boat. Bash handed him their gear, pausing briefly with narrowed eyes to watch Laura, Sarah, and Watson hike around to the other side of the lake. Their backpacks were full, and each woman carried a large flat rock with her.

"Picking berries my ass," he muttered, "she should be taking a nap."

Given Sebastian's decent mood, Drew had been hesitant to bring up his nightmare, but the ring was heavy in his pocket, and he had a few other uncomfortable questions. Bash would kill himself before laying a violent hand on Laura, but the danger was coming through his dreams. With a shudder, Drew recalled Laura's tremors and that their bedroom looked like it had been tossed by the FBI by the time he woke up. He wasn't sure if Bash would even know what he was doing if he hurt her.

Bash handed him a tackle box and, as if reading his mind said softly, "Her eyes were so dark this morning."

"She's worried," Drew said carefully, "everyone is."

"She thinks there's not enough power in her spells, but I slept better last night than I have in months." Bash lowered himself into the boat and pulled the cord to start the motor. "Did you learn anything from that ring?"

Drew pulled it from his pocket and held it up in the light. "Revenants do this when they're reaching out for vengeance."

Bash grimaced, thinking back to the revenant he and Laura fought the year before. It seemed so long ago. "That would explain how he looks."

"What your father said doesn't fit if he's already dead."

"Take everything my father says with a grain of salt," Bash dropped the anchor in the middle of the lake, "but no matter what, I can tell you that Nick's definitely dead inside."

They settled into a silent but comfortable cadence of casting and reeling, catching nothing but happy nonetheless just to be there.

On the shore, a small creature lit on a tree stump and tilted its head; watching them as they fished and judging their inability to swoop in and dive for their catch. If they'd seen it at all the men might have thought it was a hawk of some kind, but the thing spying on them was not of the natural world at all. Not theirs anyway.

Its featherless wings sat low on its back, encircling an emaciated short body which had a sickly green hue. It studied them with eyes that looked like dark crystals set deep in their sockets and reached up with long furry fingers to scratch between two tiny sharp horns on its head. When Bash steered the boat toward the shallows, three rows of sharp teeth spread into a wide, mischievous grin.

Laura and Sarah had spent the night before texting back and forth across the cabin as the men slept. They were working on their most ambitious spell yet. Just before the sun rose, they included Rhonda in the chat and though she claimed to be fully against the project, she filled in their knowledge gaps and demanded that they call her as soon as they were able to report on the results.

Watson stood guard while they laid out their materials near a circle of ash tree saplings that had sprung up after the last fires tore through the area. Normally, they would never have entered a circle they hadn't created themselves, but since Michael was their target Rhonda suggested ash for its close association with the divine warrior classes. For Sebastian's sake, they would take their chances with the residents of the space, though if it were a portal to somewhere weird, they were totally screwed.

Laura fastened the black stone necklace Daniel had given her around her neck and stepped inside the circle of trees. She felt like a hypocrite after discarding the stone at his feet when he threatened to kill Sarah, but he'd since given it back to her, and it was an angel's talisman, which was required for summoning their kind.

"What's the worst that can happen?"

Sarah gaped at her. "Why would you even say that

out loud?"

She touched the protective smokey quartz that hung at her own throat and followed her sister into the clearing. Though they weren't zapped into another dimension, magic seeped into their pores as it flowed between the trees. They were overwhelmed with power but had sense enough to know that it wasn't theirs and quickly presented the offering they'd prepared earlier of frankincense and roses.

The circle sealed around them as their gift was accepted and a worried Watson paced like a sentry on the outside. Once it became clear that they were welcome in the space, Laura used anointing oil to draw a sigil in the dirt. According to Rhonda, it was Michael's symbol and as the sunbeams dappling through the ash leaves gathered and focused directly into its center, they knew she had been right.

It annoyed them that they had to jump through such hoops to reach others of their kind. The hard truth was that being half angel did more to hurt their cause, more to hurt them in general than anything else ever had, but up to that point, communication had been the least of their worries. Thomas wasn't even on their speed dial, so Michael surely felt he owed nothing to those he considered to be abominations of his realm.

Laura was relying heavily on the fact that he'd helped them before, even if it was only to collect his accursed Thromluí. As far as she was concerned, the angels could think what they wanted about her origins, but Sebastian had done nothing but show up time and again to answer their calls. He suffered cruelly and she wasn't entirely sure she hadn't made things worse by trying to help him. She didn't know what to expect but proceeding as if she at least had the same rights to an angel as any random Catholic, hoped for the best.

Even with their genetics, summoning an archangel was bound to be draining so they crushed Fairy Duster flowers in their palms and drew protective symbols on their skin with the pink pollen. That would stabilize their nervous systems and enable them to process any intense energetic stimulation without disrupting the spell.

Michael's element was fire, but it had been a while since the last monsoon rainstorm so the danger to the forest was high. Rather than a wood fire that could get away from them, they built up a circle of rocks and piled in a few twigs with the leaves they'd cleared from the area. It wasn't much, but they wouldn't need it to burn for long. Laura flicked the phosphorescent polish on her nails to light the mulch and they sat cross legged in the dirt.

Sarah pulled their mother's book from her backpack and caught Laura smiling at her. "What are you thinking?"

They hadn't done magic together since the spell to engage Adira and before that it had been years.

"I don't know if this is going to work, but I'm glad you're here with me."

Sarah was not the sister who cried easily, but her eyes teared up. Laura always seemed to think that Sarah merely tolerated her and to be fair, Sarah's actions, particularly of late, tended to emphasize that. But Laura would never know how terrified Sarah was of losing her sister and how tending to the strength of their bond had lately become, not just a priority of hers, but a solemn vow.

Fearing that any response would bring her fully to tears, she only smiled back and flipped to the page in their mother's book where she'd found the angel summoning spell. Brona's goal was to make contact with any angel who could help her achieve a normal life, but she had learned the hard way that it wasn't just Heaven's angels who were listening in.

Laura was much more specific in her choice of words and since they'd already seen the Dream Master, they were less concerned about being taken in by a demonic imposter. Still, short of salting the forest floor, they deployed every precaution they could think of, and some that Rhonda had thought of for them.

They visualized Sebastian and Michael together and as they worked the spell, the summoning herbs began to swirl around, slowly rising to blend with the smoke from their little fire. The sunbeams mingled with the elements as they filtered up through the leaves of the ash trees which swayed from side to side even though there was no breeze in the clearing.

To close the spell, Sarah tossed a desert rose in the center of the fire and Laura's hopes soared. They felt for a moment as if they'd connected to something rare and otherworldly. Soon though, the air in the clearing seemed to thin, leaving them gasping for breath and then there was nothing. When the desert rose popped apart, the fire went out and the light that shone on Michael's sigil dimmed.

Laura's shoulders sagged and Sarah let the tears fall on her sister's behalf. "It was worth a try," she said softly.

They drowned and stirred the embers and plucked out the remains of the desert rose, sealing them in a small drawstring bag.

"I don't know why I thought it would work, but I'm still grateful for all of this."

"For what?" Sarah was incredulous. "That we were born to a couple of monsters and then turned into indentured servants?"

"Or...and hear me out," Laura sat once again in a meditative pose, "for our kids and our lovers and our friends and, believe it or not, for the magic."

High above them, the pale green creature chewed on a pinecone and watched while the witches grounded themselves after the spell. Unable to bear the sensation as their magic circulated through the air around his perch, he cast his eyes toward the men docking their boat on the shore. For the moment they were the easiest targets, but when the witches left the circle, he would be back for them.

Chapter Eleven

They tied up the boat to a felled tree, startling a squirrel who chittered his annoyance at them. "Sorry buddy," Bash said.

Drew scanned the area using his hand to shield his eyes from the sun. "I don't see the women anymore," He worried.

"Picking berries, my ass," Bash repeated, concern underlying his harsh tone. "Hey, what's that?"

Across the meadow, the pale green creature pushed off his perch and flew in their direction.

Drew took a step forward. "It's too big to be a hawk. Is it a...a little...dragon?"

"Oh, no." As it got closer, Bash could make out the horns and talons and the rocks it carried. "Get down!"

They dove in opposite directions as it soared over them, catching Drew in the forehead with a shower of rocks. Bash drew his pistol, but as he rolled onto his back, the thing sank its claws into his wrist, knocking the gun from his hand. It opened its jaws and tried to bite down on his arm, but the rows of teeth bounced off the power within Laura's shield bracelet. Bash grabbed its spindly leg with his free hand and bounced it off the ground until it released him.

He picked up his gun and chased the thing into the trees, not realizing that there was a ravine on the other side of the meadow.

"Shit!"

Teetering on the edge, he'd seen it with just enough time to stop himself from going over, but the green thing swooped in and knocked him off what remained of his balance. The rocks Bash tried to grab on the way down were slippery with moss and he found himself tumbling end over end, wondering miserably what waited for him at the bottom.

In a final effort to stop his fall, he reached out for anything. Expecting, at best, another slimy rock, he was stunned when someone appeared in midair and snatched his hand. He looked up to see Daniel hovering over him.

"What the hell?"

"Come on, Cowboy." Thomas appeared at his other side and lifted him from underneath the arms. Together, the angels carried him back to the top of the ravine where Drew looked over in astonishment.

Bash flopped on the grass and felt around for damage. Remarkably, nothing was broken, but he would be a walking bruise within a few hours. Assuming he had a few hours.

"Don't tell me that was a dragon, Daniel, because I cannot deal with medieval shit today."

"How about some demonic shit?" Thomas pumped his eyebrows.

Bash glared at him and reached around for whatever

was poking him in the back. "Well, at least I'm used to that."

"You were attacked by a Messenger Imp. It's probably been spying on you for a while."

A thin stream of blood dribbled into Drew's eye from where the rocks had cut his forehead.

"Messenger Imp?" He squinted and wiped it away with the bottom of his t-shirt.

"They gather and share information," Thomas continued, "and they wreak havoc, of course – just because they can."

"Gather information for whom?" Drew sat next to Bash, picked part of a prickly pear cactus from his back, and handed it to him.

"They work for the highest bidder," Thomas leaned over and flicked some pine needles out of Bash's collar, "and imagine my surprise, Cowboy, to learn that you're actually worth quite a bit."

"Well, message received." Bash made a face and tossed the cactus aside. "Thanks." He rose to his knees. "I'm lucky you were there, I guess."

As he and Drew helped each other to their feet, he paused. "Wait a minute, why *are* you here?"

Drew rubbed the bridge of his nose. "And why are you together?"

"I have some valuable information for you," Thomas jutted his chin at Daniel, "but he's only here to be a tattletale."

Unfazed, Daniel said. "Are you aware that Laura and Sarah have summoned Michael?"

Bash ran a hand through his hair and brought it down full of dead leaves. "*The* Michael?"

"The spell was impressive," Thomas beamed with

pride, "their powers are growing stronger all the time. In a few years, they will be—"

"It's not going to work," Daniel interrupted.

Up to that point, Michael was the only angel who had impressed Bash, but he couldn't imagine why Laura would reach out to him.

"Are you sure?"

Drew slapped his forehead with realization, then winced from the pain. "For you, Bash – he's the Dream Master." He was annoyed with himself for not thinking of it sooner. "Why wouldn't it work? People summon angels all the time."

Daniel nodded. "Yes, but the Deanes should manage their expectations."

"Oh, right. That's not how it works for us. Apparently, nothing works for us," Drew sneered. "Make sure you let Sarah know you've been travelling with Thomas." It wasn't three months earlier that Daniel tried to kill her for doing the same thing, and Drew was going to be bitter about that for a long time.

Bash pulled his pistol again as Daniel turned to leave. "Daniel, stop!"

"I'm not going to hurt them; I just thought you should know what they've been trying to do."

The coiled rattlesnake by the angel's feet arched up and hissed.

"Daniel, stop!" Bash yelled again, "Snake!"

As it sprang from the ground, fangs bared and aiming for Daniel's throat, the angel reached out and snatched it from the air, squeezing its head between his fingers.

Drew and Bash held their ears as the voice of the snake invaded their minds. "I almost had you,

Belteshazzar."

Thomas peered down at the reptile and then up at the others, "That's not a snake."

Looking closer, they observed that while it did have the body of a rattlesnake and probably fangs full of deadly poison, there were two sets of horns on top of its head. It wrapped its body around Daniel's forearm and, as he pressed his fingers tighter, its color shifted from brown to blue to a deep emerald green, and the horns lengthened several inches in its defense.

Daniel studied Bash and Drew who stood, eyes wide and gaping as he held tightly to the slithering demon. Over thousands of years, he'd learned to create a barrier between himself and his Defenses by treating them with such cold indifference that if they thought about him at all, it was only to ponder his connection to a higher power. Until then they simply did as they were told and their obedience was usually out of fear. The lack of connection saved him from hundreds of heartaches when the inevitable finally came. But if he was honest, he knew deep down that it also contributed to countless failures and unknowable collateral damage.

There was something about these men and the Deane sisters though that put them under his skin. They had told him once that they would serve his cause, but not alongside of him until he had paid his dues. By dues they meant he must act as one of them and become part of their team. But to do so meant opening his heart to them the way they did for each other, and that meant opening himself up to what he remembered as indescribable pain.

Still, Sebastian had just tried to save his life and the way Daniel had warmed over the past year to that awkward, self-destructive man was no different than how he had warmed to the obstinate witch that the man loved. For the first time in eons, he could admit that not only did he crave companionship, but he also craved theirs specifically.

"What will you do to it?" Drew wanted to know that, and even more so, he wanted to know why the demon called him Belteshazzar. The marks around Daniel's wrist were similar to the ones on Thomas, though not red and inflamed like his. Drew scrutinized the marks as the angel held up the snake and sucked in a sharp breath. Daniel was marked with the image of a lion's body and there were tiny paw prints on either side of it.

He held the demon out to Thomas, who shook his head. "I'm not taking it back there."

"You're not safe here either, Watcher. Jaya comes for all of you," the snake hissed, "and she brings an army with her."

Daniel held the snake up to his lips and blew air into its face. His breath was so cold that Drew and Bash took several steps backward to escape it. The demon spat curses into their minds and thrashed violently as, inch by inch, its body froze. Once it hardened into a solid mass, Daniel slammed his arm against a tree, shattering the snake into hundreds of icy shards.

Thomas slapped him on the shoulder, "See, you do know how to have fun!"

"Jaya?" An uncomfortable feeling washed over Bash.

Daniel shook the remaining bits of frozen snake from his hands. "You know of her?"

"Adira said she's done something to my brother."

"Well," Thomas shrugged, "that's the other reason we're here."

Bash pulled out his phone but there was no signal, so he turned to Drew. "Come on, we've got to find them first."

After shoving Sebastian down the ravine, the Messenger Imp known as Gaab circled back to find his primary targets. He was told the men were expendable, but the witches were to remain unharmed. For them, he had an offering – and an invitation.

Laura was quiet as they left the magic circle, demoralized by the failure of her spell and her inability to help Bash in general. Sarah allowed her to stew in self-pity for a few minutes and then interrupted her thoughts.

"Maybe Michael is busy right now. You know how low we are on their priority list."

Laura laughed and slung her backpack over her shoulder. "I wonder how long Mom had to wait for Thomas?"

Sarah opened her mother's book, flipped back to the summoning spell, and read aloud. In the margins of the page, Brona had written, "I looked up and he was standing in the doorway, tall and terrifying and nothing like I'd imagined. I felt the pull of him instantly."

Laura stuck her finger down her throat, pretending to retch and Gaab took the opportunity to catch them unguarded. He dove in, pulling Laura's hair and knocking the book from Sarah's hands.

"Hey!"

Watson stood in front of Laura, barking as Gaab

circled overhead.

"Good god, what is that?"

Pleased with himself, Gaab took another pass, but Watson was ready and jumped at him. He latched onto one of the little demon's feet and pulled him to the ground, screeching and furiously flapping his wings.

"Release me, hellhound!" Gaab slashed at the dog with his claws, but Watson tossed his head from side to side, disorienting the demon and slicing into the tendons that attached the foot to his bony leg.

"Watson, watch me!"

Laura rubbed her hands together and he kept his eyes on her, awaiting instructions as she gathered static electricity from the air. But as he slowed his head shake, Gaab flapped his wings and jerked his body upward, letting out a deafening squeal as his foot came away from his leg.

"You're not very bright, are you?"

Laura wrapped him in a net of static electricity and Sarah extended her arm, using her mind to throw him against the trunk of a pine tree. Watson dropped the severed foot next to Laura at the base of the tree and she rewarded him with a vigorous neck rub using her free hand.

"You did good, sweet boy."

"What do you want with us?" Sarah narrowed her focus and pushed more air out of his lungs.

Gaab ceased his struggle against their powers, whimpering, "Jaya sends me with a gift for her sisters."

They looked at each other. *Sisters?* The demon pulled a drawstring bag from a small pouch around his waist and held it out to them.

"We're not touching that." Laura tightened the

electric net and he squealed again, dropping the bag.

"She means you no harm – not yet," he gasped. "She invites you to fight for her. Come and serve as generals in her army as she rights an old and terrible wrong." He bent his head toward the bag on the ground. "A gift to show good faith. A psychic stone to help you locate the ones you love the most. See where they are and see what they do."

Sarah held up her phone, "We have GPS for that."

Gaab purred through his rows of teeth, "Learn how they feel."

Feel? Curiosity got the best of Sarah, and she picked up the bag. It was light, but magic pulsed from within. She emptied the stone into her palm and Gaab hit the ground with a thud, only Laura's net of electricity held him in place.

"Are you crazy? Leave it alone." Laura said the words, but she too was curious. "Help me keep an eye on him, Watson."

The dog hulked over the demon while Laura watched Sarah turn the stone over in her hands.

It was raw with jagged edges, but it shimmered in the sunlight with colors of green they'd never seen before, as if an opal had somehow bred with an emerald. Right away Sarah could see the faint image of Drew in the meadow. Her breath came in short, panicked bursts as she noticed the blood on his shirt and his forehead.

"Andrew is hurt."

"It's lying to you, Sarah. Put it down."

"He's bleeding."

She almost ran from her sister to find him, but then she felt the real power of Jaya's gift. The barrage of emotions that coursed through Andrew settled on top of her own and brought her to her knees. Drew's feelings were uncontained and scattered throughout his heart, overwhelming and exhausting him. She knew it was always like that for him and it was how he connected so easily with others.

Feeling everything, all the time, he had no choice but to empathize instantly with everyone he met. In the forefront of his heart that day was worry. She looked around him and spotted the angels with a disheveled Bash. *What?* Drew was worried about his friend and about her, and though his demeanor was relatively calm, he was only just keeping it together.

The banshee began to wail again, low and shrill in the back of her mind. She looked up at Laura but was more certain than ever that the wailing wasn't for her sister any more than it was for Drew. As the vision faded, she returned the stone to its drawstring bag and drew an uneasy breath for Bash.

Wings askew, the Messenger Imp scooted next to his foot, through a puddle of his own blood. He wouldn't be following them for a while so Laura released him from the static electricity and warned him, "Leave us alone."

Gaab picked up his foot and shook it at them as they left him sitting in the dirt. "You know the way to the Other Side. You will join her there, or she will come and kill you here."

Chapter Twelve

The hair stood up on their arms when they came across the circle of ash trees where Laura and Sarah had worked their spell. You didn't have to be a witch to feel the magical residue that hung in the air.

"They weren't the only ones here." Thomas said as he plucked Gaab's little claw foot from some surface tree roots, holding it up for the others to see.

Bash frowned and picked the nametag from Watson's collar out of a pool of green blood. He wiped it on his pants, dropped it in his pocket and scanned the area, shouting, "Laura!"

They fanned out and called their names for several minutes before Laura finally heard them and grabbed Sarah's arm.

"That's Bash."

They listened hard and then followed the voices until they found the men tramping through the forest with Daniel and Thomas.

"Oh, my god, the stone wasn't lying." Sarah ran to Drew and smoothed his hair away from the drying blood on his brow. "You could have a concussion."

"I'll be alright."

Ignoring him, she yanked open her backpack to get first aid, but he pulled her close for a long hug, sighing heavily as they relaxed into each other. "I think I'm better already."

Thomas made a gagging noise, but Daniel shushed him while nodding at Laura, who was glaring at them both.

"What did you do?" She eyed Bash's torn clothes and the bruises forming along his jawline and flicked her fingernails to fill her hands with fire.

"Baby, wait," Bash could not believe he was about to defend them, "they saved me from a bad...from a really bad fall."

The banshee hummed again in the back of Sarah's mind and she swallowed hard, refocusing her attention on Drew.

"By the way," Bash took Laura's hands as she reluctantly extinguished the fire, "what were you thinking, trying to summon an archangel for me?"

"I messed up the spell anyway," she looked up at him, "and it didn't work."

He touched her cheek. "We'll figure something out. We always do."

"Can't you do something about the dreams?" She pleaded with Daniel, "Michael showed up for Thromluí. Why won't he help us now?"

"Thromluí is of his realm, but Sebastian is not." Daniel was moved by her love for him, but unable intervene on his behalf.

They left the ring of trees and discovered a creek running along the far edge of Chuck's property, so they stopped there to dangle their feet in the icy water and clean up their various wounds.

Daniel settled in on one side of Laura and said, "You could have practiced your spell to summon me."

"Don't take this the wrong way, but things tend to get worse for us when you're around so...hey," she put her hands on her hips, "why *are* you here?"

Thomas sat on her other side and pushed her hair behind her ears, stroking her temples. "The symbol that insidious troll branded you with is part of a spell."

She crawled away from them and sat between Bash's legs as he rested against a thick pine tree.

"The Watchers were sent to look after the first humans, and we did that by living amongst them and sharing our knowledge." Thomas rubbed at the ugly red scars on his wrists. Once they were beautiful bands of knotwork indicating that he was created to do magic, but they'd been burned off during *the punishment*. His scars were meant to be reminders of the consequences of his poor choices, but in the centuries that followed, he grew certain that his sentence, and definitely that of the humans involved, was outsized for the so-called crimes that were committed.

"Jaya has that knowledge, and she's seen it put to its worst, most destructive uses." He leveled his gaze on Bash, "Your brother was caught up in her plans and you need to understand that even if he escapes with his life, Nicholas will never be the same."

"Why did he leave this with us?" Drew handed him Nick's ring.

Thomas studied it for a while and then shook his head. "This is a warning to anyone who would cross her."

"She claims to be our sister." Laura folded her arms and glared at Thomas, specifically sympathetic all of a sudden to Sebastian's family problems. "How many of us are there?"

"Oh, calm down," Thomas rolled his eyes, "she is like you, but she is not mine. All your other siblings were boys and they've long since perished."

Laura dropped her arms. "Is that supposed to make me feel better?"

Thomas shrugged. "No."

"She is one of the very first Nephilim," Daniel explained.

"Wait," Drew raised his hands, "I thought they fought each other until there were none left."

"She is powerful enough to have survived that, and clever enough to have escaped the flood, but she's been trapped on the Other Side all this time. She's waited centuries for the chance to escape and she believes you two," Daniel nodded at Laura and Sarah, "are the answer, since you're finally old enough to be of use to her."

Sarah laughed. "Finally?"

"Yes, you're finally growing into your power as witches...and as women. If the three of you joined forces, the effects would be..." he shuddered and left his sentence unfinished.

"That's why you're always looking for a reason to kill us."

Thomas unexpectedly came to Daniel's defense. "We didn't know she was still alive until now."

"Well," Drew was growing impatient, "it's your language so tell us what all of this means."

"I didn't write the spell," Thomas shifted

uncomfortably, "and this is only a fragment. Jaya's gone mad for revenge, but there's no human alive now who could be blamed for what she went through. There never was."

"She sent that little green thing to give us this." As soon as the stone touched Sarah's palm, an image appeared before her of Audi in Drew's house with Daphne. "Oh," tears leapt into her eyes as she was overwhelmed by the confusion and heartbreak that had been consuming her daughter.

"Let me see that." Thomas took it from her and held it up in the fading afternoon sunlight. "Stones like this used to litter the ground, but they were washed away. Can you imagine the power that used to simply...exist?"

"It's quite a gift," he dropped it into the bag and handed it back to her. "I don't have to remind you to proceed with caution."

"She also invited us to fight for her," Laura admitted, "and said she'd come for us if we declined."

"I would have been disappointed if she didn't." Bash closed his eyes, and his stomach growled loudly enough for everyone to hear. "Are we still having beef stew tonight? I'm starving."

She nodded and helped him up. It was their night to cook, and they had made a double batch of stew at home to reheat over the firepit outside of the cabin. He first rose to his knees and then stood with a groan, raising his arms overhead for a full body stretch.

"Tomorrow's gonna have to be a rest day whether I want one or not," he tapped Drew on the shoulder, "so we should hike back now and get the boat."

"No, sir," Laura picked up her backpack, "we'll get

it—Watson, do you want to go for a boat ride, sweet boy?"

"You two are in no condition to go trapsing back through the forest," Sarah agreed, hoisting her own pack on her shoulder, "it's at least two miles away and besides, if that one footed little prick is still out there..."

"Thomas and I will get the boat," Daniel announced, setting off in that direction.

All of them, including Thomas, blinked at him, and Bash rubbed at his goatee, unsure of what to say.

"Um...thanks?"

Thomas's mouth had been watering since they'd said the words beef stew, so he waved him off and trotted after Daniel. "I'm not doing this for you, Cowboy. We're starving, too, and if any of you go for the boat, dinner will be significantly delayed."

* * *

"Meditation?" Drew found Laura sitting cross legged on the living room floor in front of a thick leather-bound book.

"Kegels, actually."

He lowered his head and smiled with a blush, unsure if she was kidding or not. They didn't spend much time alone together anymore but when it happened he was reminded of how much he genuinely liked her. He only had brothers—and thanked God for that as his parents would have surely destroyed a girl—but Laura put her trust in him from the beginning, welcoming him into Chuparosa and folding him into her family. In his heart, she would always be his sister.

He was trying to decipher the angelic symbols on

Nick's ring, and had come to ask if he could, once again, inspect the mark on her temple. But looking down, he noticed that she was writing in the book.

"Laura, is this...is this your grimoire?"

She nodded, "I'm making notes about Michael's spell before I forget."

He sat next to her. "May I?"

She scooted over to give him access and as he turned the heavy, clothlike pages, he felt her essence within them. There were dozens of spells, but it was what she'd written in the margins that fascinated him most. It was why she'd worked the spells, what she'd learned, and her feelings at the time that made it like peeking into a diary.

The first pages consisted of basic protection 'how to' written in the curly script of a teenage girl with a short attention span. Love notes to Simon Le Bon and Parker Stevenson took up almost as much space. Later she became more focused, but throughout, there were plenty of pages like the one that day, where her handwriting scrawled with disappointment and frustration.

"I should probably get a new one," she said, gingerly closing the cover, "but Rhonda gave me this book decades ago."

They helped each other to their feet and went outside where Bash was adding logs to the firepit underneath an enormous Dutch oven that hung from a tripod. He hobbled a bit, but he'd set the long wooden picnic table and opened two bottles of their favorite Bordeaux. Despite his exhausted, aching body, in that moment he could not have been happier, looking forward to a relaxing night by the fire with his friends.

In fact, he was only mildly irritated when Thomas and Daniel approached from the boathouse. They met Sarah on her way back from the only good spot for a cell signal. She and Audi had managed a short but pleasant conversation, and her hopes were high that their relationship might finally be on the mend.

They sat down to eat and a disappointed Watson, who had very much wanted to go for a boat ride, was wholly cheered by his own bowl of stew that Laura placed on the deck in front of him.

After dinner, they gathered around the fire and continued telling their stories from the day.

"Could that snake demon have killed you, Daniel?" Bash could not get over seeing the frozen shards of its body melting into the pine needles.

"Quite painfully, I'm afraid." Daniel reached out, and what they hadn't seen before were the blisters left behind where it wrapped itself around his forearm.

"Our power is limited, and what we can do depends upon our purpose."

Drew eyed the lion on Daniel's wrist again and decided to take a chance by asking him about his origins. "Can you still interpret dreams?"

Daniel closed his eyes and took a deep breath.

"You had to know that was coming." Thomas jibed.

Unwilling to be part of the impending discussion, he rose and bowed to his daughters. "Good night my darlings, I'm not interested in Q & A at this point in our relationship, but I will visit you again soon." He headed for the trees and disappeared into a dramatic flash of lightning.

"Unbelievable," Bash sniffed.

Laura began to massage his shoulders and said,

"Not really."

"Is that why you serve under Michael?" Drew asked, not wanting Daniel to get sidetracked.

Earlier in the day Daniel committed himself to opening up to them, so Drew needn't have worried.

"Yes, but I've found that it's the rarest of occasions when interpretation is actually helpful to a dreamer. Most of the time, it only creates chaos, second guessing, and misery."

"Why didn't you tell us who you were?"

"Some, like Thomas, were created in the beginning. Some, like you, were born," he gestured to Laura and Sarah, "and some are given the choice when they die. An angel called James, who was the kindest soul I'd ever known, sat in conversation with me on the longest, most terrifying night of my life. I desired to help him with his work and my wish was granted when I died."

Bash leaned forward with his elbows on his knees. He learned what he knew of Daniel's story as a seven-year-old in Vacation Bible School, from which he usually ran away. He wasn't good at memorizing verses and hated doing crafts, but depending upon the teacher, could be persuaded to sit still for story time.

He would be lured in by a good hero's tale for his entire life and among his favorites back then were those of David and Goliath and Daniel in the lions' den. The Bible was quite specific about how Daniel survived his ordeal, but as a little boy, unable to grasp the concept of faith and therefore missing the point of the story, Sebastian convinced himself that, like David in another one of his favorites, Daniel had fought those lions to a standstill.

"At first, we were the recruiters and protectors of

the Defenses and then, for reasons I may never understand, we became hunters. James was sent after Thomas, and then he was murdered in Hell."

Laura sat up straight. "Thomas killed him?"

"I thought so for a long time, but I recently learned that he was forced to watch as it happened."

They were riveted by his story, though to his thinking, there wasn't much more to tell. "Without my good friend, I grew tired and a bit...lost. There are fewer and fewer willing Defenses now and I've already lost so many of you that I tried to interact as little as possible. Against my better judgment, I can't help being particularly drawn to you, the Ruiz's, and your children. By now you know that's probably not good for any of us."

"By now *you* know that interaction is everything to us." Bash reminded him.

"Our dysfunctional functioning." Drew laughed. He respected Daniel's transparency and could appreciate his markedly human reaction to despair, especially from one who was once such a remarkable human being.

* * *

"Shhhh."

Bash put a finger to his lips as Drew and Sarah came in from an afternoon *visit* to Satan's shed. His sleep wasn't as violent after that first night in the cabin, but it was fitful, and Laura wasn't getting any rest. He'd found her napping in the living room and was debating with himself on how best to convince her that he should be sleeping on the couch until something could be done about his dreams.

"We don't know how to help each other," he whispered, "and it's driving me out of my mind."

Sarah led them back outside to talk. "She's going to rework the spell for Michael when we get back to Chuparosa and she wants you to participate next time, so don't be a dick about it."

Bash folded his arms and sulked against the deck railing thinking Laura probably hadn't mentioned that yet because she knew he'd be a dick about it. It wasn't the magic though; it was the fuss over him and the problems he wished he wasn't causing that made him so uncomfortable with the idea.

"I won't."

"Hey friends!" Angie leaned out of the window and waved as Doug pulled his truck in the driveway.

"I forgot about the cedars," Drew grinned at Sarah, "good thing we got back when we did."

"You two are gonna get eaten by bears," Bash grumbled, "and don't come crying to me when — hey Doug! How's it goin'?"

Doug delivered a box of parts for Drew and retrieved two mini chainsaws from the bed of his truck, handing one to Bash. "Between the two of us, this shouldn't take long."

"It's a beautiful day, do you and Laura want to go for a hike?" Angie asked, already hoisting her backpack to her shoulders.

There was no way she would be able to sleep through the chainsaws, so Sarah agreed on her sister's behalf, just as Laura opened the door to say hello. Her eyes were so dark that Angie had to stifle a gasp, but Laura would never turn down the opportunity to hike a forest trail. Within a few minutes she'd poured herself a tumbler of iced coffee and was ready to go.

"There's no service out there, Ange," Doug warned, "so be careful."

"It's okay, the trailhead's not far and we have a map." She held it up for him to see.

Bash observed that her map was upside down and as they headed for the trail, Doug gave him a pained look and said, "That does not comfort me."

Watson ran to Laura's side and turned to the men as if to say, "I got this."

The women getting lost was the least of Sebastian's worries, but he decided not to trouble Doug with that information.

It was a long, sweaty afternoon but eventually what remained of the cedars were piled into the back of Doug's truck. Inside, Bash handed out beers and they gathered with Drew around the kitchen table underneath the newly restored lights.

"Is there any more of that Chex mix?"

Bash's hunger had no off switch in the higher elevation and they'd been working hard, so he was ravenous. At best, Drew's cooking skills were limited, but he could make anything with cereal. Chex Mix was a favorite along with the Rice Krispie treats to which Drew's addition of chocolate chips elevated them in Bash's mind to nothing less than gourmet.

While they gobbled up the last of the snacks, Doug glanced at the end of the table where Drew had been attempting to decipher the angelic spell. It was none of his business, so he tried to ignore it, but he'd spent so much time in the church that some of what was written jumped out at him.

Drew caught him staring and asked, "Do you recognize any of this?"

"Only what you wrote about the evil eye," he hesitated, but they looked so hopeful he decided to share some of his past. "The church I used to belong to was obsessed with that sort of thing, but they thought it was satanic," he looked out the window for any sign of Angie, "they thought everything was satanic."

Drew showed him Nick's ring. "The language is circles within circles and in the spaces between are symbols for various things," Doug appeared to be following, so he continued, "we know the ring contains a warning, and that this," he showed him his phone, "is part of a spell." Laura had banned all further physical inspection, so he was using a picture he'd taken of the brand on the side of her head.

Doug's jaw tightened. "Who did this to her?"

"That's a really long story," Bash said, "just know that we took care of him."

Thinking back to Laura's grimoire, Drew said, "Spells are like recipes with ingredients and instructions. It looks like she was branded with the ingredient list, so the instructions must be on the way."

He found himself looking out the window as well. "I need to keep a close eye on Sarah."

"The symbol in the first rung on Laura's mark matches the shape of the turquoise in the ring," Doug offered, "and around here, people believe that turquoise connects Heaven and earth."

Bash ran his finger over a triangle with a wavy line through it in the second circle. "That's air or maybe wind, and I think that one is blood," he rubbed his eyes and squinted at the fourth symbol, "but this looks like the bullshit emoji to me."

Drew laughed and held it up. "A pot, or a vessel?"

"I think it's supposed to be clay."

Bash blinked and then smiled to himself, realizing that Doug, who was covered in red clay dirt every day of his life would naturally be the one to work that out for them. Even so, their new friend was just a little too comfortable with the subject at hand, and it was making him nervous. "This stuff isn't weird to you?"

Leaving a thin film of dust on the chair, Doug stood with his back to them and looked out the window again.

"We, uh, we have some magical friends and...not too long ago, Angie..." he heaved a sigh of relief, spotting first Watson and then the women as they returned from their hike, "...she was almost burned alive."

Bash sat back in his chair. "Jesus Christ, Doug."

"It's another really long story, but I told you that you'd have to work hard to sound crazy to me."

Chapter Thirteen

Daphne's eyes darted suspiciously from the pet carrier to Audi, who was packing up her litter box and some food. The energy in Drew's house had become overpowering and Audi couldn't keep the unsettling visions out of her head when she was there, so his cat would be going home with her until he returned.

There was a knock at the door and through the peephole, she saw Cara Marshall holding a small boom box and an enormous tote bag full of what appeared to be a thrift store haul.

She opened the door and shoved an indignant Daphne into the carrier. "What's all this?"

"Some decorations for Laura's party," Cara grinned, "and would you believe that most of it came from my closet?"

Having recently moved her mother's Gen-X shrine of a closet, Audi had no problem believing that. She poked around at the top of the tote bag and pulled out a dozen cassette tapes, a few yards of neon tulle, three Rubik's cubes, and a black light.

"Look," Cara unrolled a poster and flicked the black light on it, revealing a skeleton with long green hair holding a guitar. "I thought Andrew would appreciate this."

"What? Why?" Audi made a face. "What is that thing?"

"It's Eddie…Iron Maiden's mascot."

"I don't understand those words in the order you used them but come on in."

Cara hesitated and Audi smacked her forehead. "Oh shit, I forgot."

"I still forget sometimes too, but Andrew hasn't invited me in since I…changed." Cara had no regrets about allowing Adam to make her a vampire, but she and her friends were still coming to terms with a lot of the details.

Audi put the decorations inside and sat next to Cara on the porch bench.

"Is it scary?"

She had so many questions for Cara since learning her story, but they hadn't spent enough time together for her to ask.

Cara nodded her head. "Daytime scares me. I don't want to die like that."

Audi shuddered thinking that, though the possibility was fairly remote, every woman she knew was in danger of burning to death for one reason or another.

"Are you on your way out to…" she wasn't sure how to finish her sentence without sounding silly, but Cara laughed and waved her off.

"I'm a very, very picky eater so it's a good thing I only have to go out a couple of times a month."

Audi gulped. "Do blood types taste different?"

"They do, but that's not what I meant." Something dark passed over her eyes and she said, "There are some terrible people out there and they taste the best...to me anyway."

Audi arched an eyebrow. "I don't know if I could do it." Even if Cara was hunting bad guys, that aspect of the lifestyle was a nonstarter for her.

"I didn't know what I was capable of until I met Adam." They both knew that was a lie. Cara was one of the many formidable women in Audi's life, and no matter how much she loved Adam, she never would have agreed to the change if she wasn't certain she could do it.

Still, there was another burning question that Audi wanted the answer to. Adam had never shown her anything but kindness, but by the ferocity with which he tore into their enemies she knew that he would stop at nothing if the fight was important to him. If Cara had seen that part of him before she made her decision, was she afraid that he would come after her, or her friends, if she left him?

"He didn't force you, did he?"

"No, he didn't." Cara was quiet for a moment and then in a low, hard voice that chilled Audi's bones, she said, "And, it turns out that Adam is a much better person than I am."

As she puttered around getting Daphne situated at her house, it occurred to Audi that though Sarah was close to them, Cara and Mena were technically Laura's friends from high school. If Sarah had old friends like that of her own, they'd fallen away once she had a family and

Audi again felt a pang of compassion for her mother. She didn't believe Sarah regretted having a family but wondered how many choices within *that* choice she would make differently, if given the chance.

She felt Brian in her head just before her phone rang. He and Becky were meeting a chemist friend who had agreed to analyze one of Fiona's spell vials. Her grandmother's van had been full of foul things, but before they set it on fire, she and Becky each took a vial labeled "solution." Fiona heavily relied on poisons in her craft, and the vial could have held an antidote of some kind, but they needed to know the ingredients to be sure.

He put her on speaker phone and reminded the chemist not to touch the liquid. "And don't get it on anything else either."

"Oh, crap, it burned through the desk mat."

There was a small ruckus on the other end of the phone and then she heard Brian say, "I literally just told you..."

"Okay, okay. We'll take this to the computer and be right back."

When Becky and the chemist left the room, Audi quizzed her cousin on a subject she knew he had been dreading. "Did you tell them yet?"

"Becky wants to wait until they get here."

Audi rolled her eyes. "I'll put that on your tombstone. Or better yet, 'here lies the dumbest man ever.' Which one do you like best?"

"Very funny."

"You don't have to decide because your body will be in multiple pieces when Sheriff Scott gets done with you, so I'll be able to use as many tombstones as I want." She felt a sensation just then that was akin to how the first sip of hot cocoa hits your system on a chilly afternoon.

"Hang on, Rhonda's here." She opened the door and put her phone on speaker. "Come on in, Brian says 'hi.' They're analyzing that stuff we found in Fiona's van."

Rhonda kissed her forehead and handed her a bag of late season lemons from one of her trees. "And?"

She and Audi sat at the table and listened as Becky and her friend returned with a list of ingredients.

"Everything's floating in castor oil, but you've got cayenne pepper, habanero seeds, cactus thorns...oh, and a dead wasp."

"All bottled up with a whole bunch of nasty intentions." Audi said with a low whistle.

That potion would not have been an antidote to anything, rather it was likely one of the darkest of her grandmother's spells.

"Brian, you seal that up and put it away somewhere safe," Rhonda warned, "my mother made a similar potion she called 'ailing oil' and sold it to local women who were being stalked or beaten or...worse. She told me it ails what haunts you."

"I will." Brian said. He was already sealing the bottle into an empty stainless-steel thermos that he would store with the other things they recovered from Fiona's trailer.

Those particular items could not be burned, buried or otherwise disposed of without risking harm to an innocent person, so they became his responsibility for the rest of his life. The ominous duty added to his sense of purpose and made him feel more like an adult, which he'd struggled with during his last years of college.

He'd been frustrated by the desire to get started with his life and was finally beginning to feel that things were falling into place for him.

"I've gotta cleanse the lab and get to the pool."

"Good luck at your meet and," Audi grinned at Rhonda, "with everything else."

* * *

Flagstaff was not at all close to Pinetop, but the drive to I-40 was beautiful and in a little over two hours the vacationers successfully convoyed from Chuck's cabin to Northern Arizona University.

Brian missed several practices during his family's summer battles with Fiona and the troll, and since his scholarship was tied to the swim team, he had subsequently been placed on both athletic and financial probation. However, that morning was to be the last swim meet of his senior year, so afterward he would be free to come and go as he pleased, and he intended to do just that.

Drew nearly tackled him with a hug outside of the aquatics building. Brian had been a sullen teenager when they met, but they'd bonded over shared careers in electricity and then Drew found himself happily taking on the role of a much older brother to the boy. He was as proud as Laura of Brian's accomplishments, and she was grateful that her son was so comfortable with one of the men she trusted with their lives.

"So, what's the word?" Drew knew that he had applied for an electrical engineering job with a local contractor and that there was some doubt because of his age, but Brian's ear to ear grin told him all he needed to know. He pumped his fist and said, "Yes!"

Becky, who had been trapped in one of her father's bear hugs, wriggled away when Watson jumped out of the Jeep. Everyone stared as she knelt in front of him with her arms held out. She'd once been badly bitten by a large dog and was terrified of Watson when they first met, but Brian drew their attention to her wrist.

"I made her a shield bracelet like the ones mom made for you guys."

Bash and Drew were saved on a handful of occasions by the magic in Laura's bracelets and knowing his daughter would enjoy the same protection, Bash felt particularly grateful to Brian just then. He had woven his magic into lavender and sage colored paracord and hung a gold, dog shaped charm from the center.

Becky proudly held up her hand for Laura's inspection and then wrapped her arms around Watson's neck. "It's not just for dogs, but isn't the charm a sweet touch? See, it's a German Shepherd."

Indeed, it wasn't just for dogs. Laura felt the strength in the energy as it pulsed from the strands of cord and when she looked at Brian to tell him so, she found she could no longer see her little boy. Though his eyes shone with the excitement of the day, the person standing tall before her had the sharp, cleanly shaven jaw of a grown man and the enlightened overall expression of a powerful witch. *When had that happened?* Half of her heart was bursting with pride while the other half shattered, and the competing emotional sensations weakened her in the knees to the point where she had to lean against the Jeep for support.

Sarah was the only one who noticed and, whether it

was a sympathetic nod to Laura's empty nest syndrome or knowing looks as it became clear that Brian and Becky were closer than anyone thought, they found themselves exchanging glances for the rest of the day.

Their form of unspoken communication was only magical in the sense that it had been cultivated over decades of shared experiences, but they were moved that day by the realization that the closeness both sisters feared was lost had returned in full force during their vacation.

After the swim meet, they met at Becky's new apartment where Laura presented her with bundles of home grown sage and piles of freeze-dried oranges doused in cinnamon.

"For a safe, happy home."

Without thinking, Brian tossed his duffel bag onto Becky's bed, eliciting a group smile from most of the older adults. Bash had not seen as he was busy inspecting the place for leaks and breaks, unaware that Brian had done exactly that when he helped her search for the apartment.

"Do you still want matching tattoos?" Becky asked. "Because my new artist is fantastic."

Bash knew there was a rose on Becky's shoulder, done to rebel against her grandmother, but that had been years ago. "I haven't seen your new tattoo."

"That's because it's on my butt."

He made a face and returned to his study of the hinges on her cabinet doors.

"What you want is easy," Becky pulled out her phone and sent a flurry of texts, "She's available today. We could make it a girls' afternoon and then get dinner with everyone else."

"I guess I don't see why not."

In truth, Laura was a bit nervous about strangers, particularly those with needles, but Becky's enthusiasm was contagious. Within minutes they had sorted it out that the men would get them checked into their hotel and then they would meet for Mexican food afterward.

On her way out, Becky squeezed Brian's hand and gave him a soft peck on the lips. Bash's mouth fell open and as the women closed the door behind them, he nearly wrenched his back spinning to face the young man.

"Are you fucking kidding me?"

Drew choked back a snort of laughter, but Bash was not amused. "Did you know about this?"

Drew shook his head, "We figured it out over the course of the day. Everyone except you, I guess."

"The first time I kissed her, I forgot my name." Brian's intent had been to impress upon the older man how much of an impact Becky had on him, but when Bash's entire body went rigid, he realized that wasn't the best sentence to start with and added quickly, "We care about each other, we have the same goals, and we get along really well."

The truth was that they fought even more than Bash and Laura did when they first started dating, but since meeting Becky, Brian had developed an appreciation that once eluded him for highly passionate relationships. Figuring it was a bad idea to burden Becky's father with those insights, he simply squared his shoulders and stood his ground.

"So, if you're gonna be mad—"

"I'm not mad, Brian." Bash paced around the tiny living room, "A head's up would've been nice though,

Jesus. Just give me a god damned minute, okay?"

Brian paced in the other direction. "Becky thought a 'ripping off the Band-Aid' approach was best."

"Well," Drew stood between them chuckling, "she left you holding that Band-Aid, my friend."

"I will be having a conversation with her about that shit." Bash said.

Looking back over the day, he was starting to see where he'd missed the obvious signs and, if he was honest, he hadn't so much missed the signs as ignored them. For the most part, Becky grew up without him and since he was determined to be a central part of her adult life, he'd known he would have to welcome any man she loved, no matter what he thought of him. That she'd chosen Brian was a stroke of luck he would not have dared to imagine so, while it would take some time to wrap his brain around the idea, he would do so cheerfully.

He stuck his hand out to shake and said, "Just keep your kissing stories to yourself, alright?

Chapter Fourteen

Except for Becky's occasional back seat directions, the three women were quiet as Sarah drove Drew's 4Runner to the tattoo shop. When they pulled in, Laura hopped out and opened Becky's door with a nervous smile.

"Your father can testify that it's not easy to be in love with one of the Deanes. God, most of the time it's not even safe," she tilted her head up to keep a tear from falling down her cheek, "but if you let us, this family will care for you like no other."

The acceptance and understanding were so far above and beyond the mere tolerance Becky expected that she lunged out of the vehicle and threw her arms around Laura.

"Personally," Sarah interrupted, "I'm reserving judgment until I'm sure this tattoo isn't going to hurt."

"Oh, it's going to hurt," Becky pushed open the shop door to the shop and grinned at her, "but that's part of the fun."

Laura and Sarah were introduced to Gail, who owned the tiny strip mall shop with her partner, Lucy.

A small tablet on the front desk acted as a point of service sales system and two salon style reclining chairs with thick arm rests took up the center of the room. Fresh daisies floated in bowls on all the tables and foliage in every shade of green cascaded from shelves lining the walls.

"It's been a slow day and we were ready to leave," Gail's smile was genuine and friendly as she settled Laura into her chair, "but when Becky texted, we decided to stick around and take your money."

Laura felt at home right away and couldn't wait to get to know them. "This is a birthday present to myself," she explained, "but I might have chickened out if Becky hadn't told us about you."

"Whatever," Sarah argued, "it wouldn't surprise me if this turned into a whole flock of hummingbirds over time."

Sarah was right. Laura was anxious, but only to get started. As she fidgeted and looked around the shop, she could have sworn she saw movement in the shadows of the back room, but Gail captured her attention by pressing down on her arm.

"You ready?"

"Do it."

Though Sarah would never have admitted it, she was afraid. It wasn't the pain but the daringness of the experience that frightened her. When Rueben was alive, a tattoo was the kind of thing she would have outwardly judged Laura for while secretly wishing she could have one herself. As was always the case when those situations arose, she was torn between feelings of resentment toward her late husband and guilt over his death.

Becky dragged the stool from behind the desk and perched near the foot end of their chairs to watch. "I read somewhere that a group of hummingbirds is called a 'charm.' Isn't that sweet?"

The process was more painful than either woman was prepared for, but less than plenty of other things they'd endured and in about thirty minutes they were holding up their wrists to compare designs. Each haloed hummingbird was roughly two inches tall, but with very different personalities, just like Laura and Sarah, and the sisters thought they were perfect.

Becky's phone beeped with a text message, and she exhaled with whoosh of relief. "Brian says it looks like Dad will recover from the shock." She looked down at her hands. "He was right. He wanted to tell you together, before you got here."

Like Bash, Laura intended to have a private conversation with Brian over the manner of their big reveal, if only to find out why he thought he had to hide it from her, but learning it was Becky's idea made her rethink that and she decided to let it go. Sarah, on the other hand, was going to make her thoughts known to the girl.

"You and Brian have to be on the same page before you do anything important, Becky." Her tone was so serious that every other woman in the room paused to listen. "At least make sure you both feel comfortable talking about what you want. Otherwise, one of you will always be wondering 'what if' and that will be the kiss of death to your relationship."

In an effort to lighten the mood, Lucy spoke up for the first time, saying, "I thought a group of hummingbirds was called a 'bouquet.'"

"Hmmm," Becky took out her phone to look it up just as Gaab flew out of the back room and dug his one clawed foot into her hair.

"Where did that come from? What is it?" Lucy turned on the needle gun, grabbed him by his stumped leg and dragged it across his narrow thigh, leaving a thick blue line. His face contorted as he squealed and jerked his body away from her.

She reached for him again, but a dark mist flowed along the floor and over her and Gail. Becky touched Lucy's arm and recoiled from the evil that emanated from her skin. "This is bad," she said, "I can feel it."

A sand-colored lizard like being, roughly the size of Watson, with a long thick tail and sharp horns slithered in her direction.

"I haven't seen one of those in a while." Laura flicked her fingernails and pulled fire into her palms but two more imps, slightly larger and much stronger than Gaab, flew from the back and pushed her against the wall, pinning her arms out from her sides. She kicked at them, and they slammed her again, knocking her head hard enough to make the room spin.

The lizard demon tossed its head from side to side, cornering Becky and drooling a trail of molten saliva that sizzled when it hit the wood floor.

Whatever had possessed Gail and Lucy turned on Sarah but, unwilling to hurt the women, she only used her power to toss a tray of tools in their direction.

"Stay back," she ordered.

Undeterred, they grabbed her by the shoulders and dragged her to the chair. She threw Gail aside, again as lightly as she could, all the while begging Lucy to stop.

Lucy's eyes glazed over, and she squeezed her hand

around Sarah's neck while Gail recovered and picked up the needle gun. Sarah screamed and thrashed until she saw spots from the increasing pressure of Lucy's grip on her throat, and then Gail tore open Sarah's blouse and began to draw.

When she was done, the mist lifted itself from the two artists and they collapsed, unconscious. The imps holding Laura released her, and though she followed them with a stream of fire, they disappeared unharmed into the storage room.

She then focused her power on the lizard demon. When it melted into the floor, Becky picked up the tray Sarah had thrown and swung it at Gaab, smacking him so hard on the backside that he tumbled end over end through the air.

"Bitch!" He wailed, and before escaping with the others, he hovered near the door and called out to them, "Jaya will meet you at the waterfall in two days."

Laura and Becky rushed to Sarah, who was slumped over in the chair trying to catch her breath. Laura wiped the blood from her chest to find a circle full of symbols tattooed just below her collar bone.

"Dammit."

Sarah leaned past Laura to take Becky's hand. "So, anyway," she coughed, "you'll never get bored in this family either."

* * *

Back home and with only one day before the scheduled meeting with Jaya, Drew and Bash invited Chuck and Adam for some nighttime target practice at the Ben Avery range. While unpacking their gear, Chuck reached into the side pocket of his duffel to retrieve a pair of glasses.

"Those new?" Bash asked.

They were new, and Chuck had been self-conscious since he'd first put them on. "I only need them to focus at night and," he warned, "if any of you laugh, I'll shoot you."

Bash took a pair from his shirt pocket and though Drew wore contacts, he pointed to the readers sitting on top of his ammo box. Even Adam held up some glasses, but he put his on with pride.

"You can't imagine how pleased I was when bifocals were invented. I got my first pair in 1956."

"You didn't get to be young again when...?" Chuck gestured to his teeth.

"I'm afraid one of the more darkly humorous aspects of my condition is that I was frozen in time well after my body left its most dignified decades behind."

Cara had told Laura that Adam was fifty-five when he became a vampire, and Bash wondered if that didn't somehow make the situation better for him. An older man carried around the expectation of wisdom and responsibility, and a certain amount of freedom came with that. If he'd been younger when he was turned, Adam might have long since tired of feeling as if there were always something to prove.

He himself found that aspect of his thirties and forties exhausting and though his fifty-one-year-old body became less cooperative each year, he was grateful for the escape from the race that his hard-won frown lines afforded him.

Unsure of what they would be up against in the coming days, they'd brought every firearm they owned and were amazed to learn that though they were all excellent shots, Adam put everyone to shame. He was still undecided about how much of his past should be revealed to his new friends, so when they stared, he simply said, "I have some skill in this area."

Watching him put away his 9mm pistol, it occurred to Bash that while Adam was an *old* miner when he became a vampire, he would have been a young man in the mid-eighteen hundreds. Just then, every wild west cowboy fantasy he'd ever had as a boy jumped to the forefront of his mind.

"You were a gunfighter."

Adam looked up with a shy grin. "They called us 'shootists' in those days." Aware that Bash was working hard to refrain from asking a million questions, he decided to open up – at least about the skills he possessed that could help them.

"I still prefer some of the old things." They gathered around to watch him measure out powder, drop a lead ball and ram it into the cylinder of a Colt Walker .44. "This one's not very accurate, but it's fun to shoot, and would you believe I paid $14.50 for it in 1865?"

It felt good to share their enthusiasm for something that had always meant a great deal to him. "It was one of the first frivolous things I ever bought for myself. I used a rifle for accuracy when I was working though. My father bought me a Henry lever action, but when I got serious, I traded it in for a Winchester 66."

Bash's expression darkened when Adam used the words 'working' and 'serious.' Since he was eight years old, he'd read everything he could get his hands on about the kind of man you had to be to live the life Adam once did.

Subconsciously, Adam had been waiting for that moment and looked him in the eyes. "Sebastian, I've been a lot of things, and a vampire is not the worst of them."

As Bash pondered the future implications of that, he reminded himself that his most cherished relationships were also the most hazardous. Rather than respond to Adam's confession, he flipped open the cylinder of his Smith and Wesson .357 to show it was unloaded, and then handed it to him.

"I bought this when I started with the county," He explained.

Adam's relief was evident and there was really nothing else to say on the matter – not yet, so he took the gun, weighed it in his hand and pointed it down range.

His interest was obviously historical, but as a left-handed man, Bash's preference for revolvers was also practical. They discussed that for a while and then Bash finally dared to ask a few other shootist related questions.

Adam was thrilled to have made a connection and for the rest of Bash's life, the two men made monthly trips to Ben Avery for night shooting.

Chapter Fifteen

"I planned to bring you to this waterfall under more romantic conditions," Sarah told Drew while loading her little .38 special. They were parked in his 4Runner near the spot where she and Laura first heard the rushing water. She shoved the gun into the holster on her backpack strap and rested her head on his shoulder as they slouched against the vehicle, waiting for the others.

Drew and Bash were furious with themselves for not being there when the women were attacked at the tattoo shop, and they were not going to let them meet Jaya alone. The four of them would hike to the falls and find out what they could about her plans while Chuck and Audi waited below to back them up.

Unwilling to take any extra chances, they'd also enlisted Noah to be there in case things went sideways. Chuck had the misfortune of driving the young ex-lovers, who did not speak at all during the trip. When they parked, Audi jumped out and trotted over to her mother.

Chuck slammed his door and complained to Noah, "That was damned uncomfortable, man."

Noah shrugged gloomily, and they went to meet Bash and Laura, who were pulling up in her Jeep.

"Might as well get some use out of these." Chuck handed out the brand-new radios that were mistakenly sent by the county.

Drew turned his over in his hands and then clipped it on his belt. "Fancy."

Chuck thumbed behind him at the young people who were keeping their distance, "I can't believe I have to sit here with Ross and Rachel."

Bash laughed and took a radio. "Other duties as assigned, my friend. Besides, Watson will keep you company."

Watson would much rather have been going with his Laura and his *big man*, but he understood his assignment, scanning the area diligently for threats.

Chuck scratched the dog behind the ears, warning, "Just be careful up there."

As they cleared the top of the ridge, their slight dizziness indicated that they'd crossed over to the Other Side and, as before, they reached the ledge to find the waterfall pouring down the mountain. Sarah peered into the cave behind the falls, but it was not the Bobs who greeted her.

Laura was five-foot-ten and Sarah was a half-an-inch taller, but the woman who stepped through the water could have stood nose to nose with Andrew at six foot two. Her clothes dried instantly, a novelty of the Other Side that they'd once experienced themselves.

Jaya was barefoot, but her outfit, though quite form-fitting, was otherwise practical for the desert. She wore tan colored cargo pants nearly identical to the pair Laura had on and a sage green tank top. A symbol very similar to the ones Laura and Sarah had recently acquired peeked over the neckline.

Her skin was brown, and several curls of her long black hair escaped a low ponytail that hung down her back. She had an airy smile and green eyes that twinkled with innocence one minute and flashed with suspicion the next. Laura frowned, thinking, so much for her theory that her own green eyes, unique in her family, meant that she was more human than angel.

Sarah leaned close to Laura's ear. "I don't know what I expected, but this is not it."

Laura approached her with less caution than Bash would have preferred, but they needed to at least appear to be in control of the meeting for as long as possible. "You're Jaya?"

Jaya nodded absently and wandered over to a Creosote bush covered with its signature yellow flowers and fuzzy white seeds. Like Laura and Sarah, she was elemental and definitely an earth witch since the plant practically leapt up to greet her.

"This is my favorite child." She crushed some of the flowers in her hand, whispered over them and gave them to Sarah. "Rub this on your part of the spell to stop the pain."

The haphazard tattoo below her collar bone had indeed been hurting, and Sarah was afraid it might be infected. Drew shifted on his feet as, to show trust, she smeared it over the wound. Not only did the pain go away, but the inflammation receded until there was nothing left but the dark blue of the ink.

It was an impressive gesture, but Laura didn't

believe for a second that she was trying to make amends. A wild energy radiated from her that they usually felt around Adira, but Jaya's aura also had an alarming component of instability.

Laura began to form a theory and followed up right away with a question that had bothered her since they learned of Jaya's existence. "You're half human like us. How have you lived so long?"

"Look around," she spread her arms wide, "there is power everywhere just waiting to be absorbed and," her voice hardened, "fantastic creatures willing to bargain to help you do it."

The unsteadiness Laura experienced when crossing dimensions had lessened each time they did it and she often wondered whether they could live on the Other Side if it ever became necessary. Watching Jaya vacillate between personalities made it clear that was not going to be an option. Laura was convinced that Jaya had been there way too long and that it had made her insane.

She seated herself on a large rock near Jaya's creosote, crisscrossed her legs and rested her elbows on her knees. "So then you're not really leaning into your human roots these days."

"Why should I when I was banished from that world?" Jaya pulled at the curls around her face and her eyes zipped back and forth as if she were a caged animal. A moment later, she smiled and sat next to Laura, crossing her legs in the same way.

"At first I didn't know what to do," she shrugged and patted the rock, inviting Sarah to sit on the other side of her, "so I waited, and I bargained, and I studied and then..." she clapped her hands, "I learned of a Watcher who escaped his prison, and that he made me sisters!" She kissed them each on the cheek. "Of course, I had to wait some more, but now you're ready."

Laura leaned away from her. "Ready for what?"

"During the next full moon," Jaya's eyes sparkled with excitement, "our powers will be at their peak for the month, but it will still take all three of us to work the spell."

"What does the spell do?" Laura asked.

Jaya rolled her head around and said sternly, "You killed my troll."

They were getting whiplash trying to follow her moods. Laura lifted her chin, ready to say she would kill him again, but Jaya waved her off. "Saved me the trouble." She picked a yellow wildflower and gave it to Sarah. "My troll told you that our kind needs a country of our own where we have room to breathe and grow."

"What does it do?" Laura asked again, losing her patience.

"We will flood the west." Jaya said proudly. "It's burning you know, and it will be uninhabitable for humans very soon. When the water recedes, we will reclaim this piece of land for ourselves." She patted their knees to soothe their obvious disbelief. "You will see that this benefits everyone."

"Killing millions of people?" Drew took a step toward her. "You're crazy."

She jumped off the rock and laid down on her belly, whispering into the dirt. The ground shifted, cracking underneath where he stood and swallowing him to his waist. She rested her chin on her hands and said, "Do not call me crazy."

"Drew!" Sarah lunged for him, but Jaya dragged her palm through the wildflowers next to her and they wrapped their stems around her knees, toppling her over.

Drew grabbed on to the edges of the cracks and hoisted himself out of the hole, mumbling to Bash, "Oh no, not crazy at all."

"The real crazy thing," Jaya stood, not bothering to dust herself off, "is that people come in droves to the desert. They come and they come, and they never stop. They'll keep coming and when they start to die of thirst, where will they go?" She held out her arms and spun in a circle. "They will swarm across the rest of your country like locusts. An unwelcome scourge, exploiting more resources that don't belong to them."

"You don't belong here, either." Sarah pulled a knife from her pocket and began to cut herself free from the wildflowers.

"Stop!" Jaya squealed and waved her hands over the flowers until they loosened their grip.

"Oh, my sisters...the things that I've endured have given me the right." Jaya paced around the creosote bush, plucking off more white fuzzy fruit capsules and dropping them into Laura's hand, "My father taken away from me in chains," she waved to no one in particular, "my village tossed in the swells." She put her hands over her ears and screamed into the sky, "Murderer!"

"You don't care about the Other Side," Laura sneered. "For all those centuries, you've just been plotting revenge."

"Justice!" Jaya screamed again, "Those who want justice will follow me."

Bash feared that Jaya was moments away from completely losing her grip, so he approached the rock where the women were gathered. "What does my brother have to do with any of this?"

Jaya looked at him as if he were a toddler interrupting an adult conversation. "Nicholas is a waste of space, but he agreed to do a job for me, and thus far has failed miserably. I should have known, but he certainly got your attention, I'll give him that."

"What did you do to him?"

She breathed an irritated sigh. "He still owes me some work and will be in his current state until he gets it done."

"Is it something I can take care of for him?"

"You can, but it won't be the same," she batted her eyelashes, "you see...he's supposed to kill you."

Laura jumped off the rock and started for Bash, but Jaya held up a hand to stop her. She walked in a circle around him, looking him up and down.

"My, my Laura, what a big brave boy you've got here. He thinks he's so in love with you but watch what I can make him do."

She pressed her hips close to his and traced her finger along his jaw. When he looked at her, his rational thoughts dissolved into a gnarled mass and his body quivered with yearning. He closed his eyes and licked his lips as she played with his mind. Then he grabbed her by the waist and pulled her to him, sliding his hand over her bottom. If he pushed Laura out of the way, he could bend Jaya over the rock and be inside of her within seconds.

His brain burned with regret as soon as the thought crossed his mind and when Jaya slipped her fingers into his hair, his stomach flipped with disgust. It was one of his favorite things that Laura did, a gesture he longed for when they were apart, and magical manipulation could never come close to the tenderness of her touch. He snatched Jaya's hand and pulled it away from his head.

"You're hard to get," she said, "not like your brother at all." She tapped the fingers of her other hand on his belt buckle and shot Laura a haughty glance. "Sebastian, why don't you tell us what you really want?"

Laura and Sarah stayed silent knowing that any move they made could get him hurt, and Drew looked at the ground, unable to watch anymore.

"I want you..." Bash squeezed down hard on her wrist and shoved her away from him, "to back the fuck off."

She stumbled away like a drunk girl in high heels and then glared down at his shield bracelet. "Ahh, that's some powerful protection you've got there."

Bash shuddered inside and out. Laura's shield had kept him from doing something awful, but just barely, and he wanted to throw up.

Laura stepped in front of him, filled one hand with fire and grabbed Jaya's ponytail with the other, dragging her in front of the creosote bush. "I'm not working that spell so if you insist on coming over, be ready for a fight." She tossed a fireball in the bush and jerked Jaya to the ground in front of it. "I'll see you on the full moon."

Jaya's maniacal screams followed them as they scrambled down the back side of the falls. When they reached the vehicles and the air was finally quiet, Laura wrapped her arms around Bash's neck.

"By the way, that bracelet is for your protection, not mine. There's no component to the spell that will keep you from having another woman if you decide to—"

"Stop it. Stop it now," his eyes reddened, and he pushed her back against the Jeep, "if you want to watch my heart break right here in real time, tell me you think I would ever, ever want someone else."

"That's not what I think, but listen to me Bash," she said, touching his face to soothe him, "I had to tell you about the bracelet, that you resisted her magic on your own, because I don't think you understand just how powerful you can be."

"She's absolutely right."

For a moment the noon sun seemed so bright that they had to shield their eyes and when it dimmed, they turned to see Michael leaning against the Jeep next to Laura.

Chapter Sixteen

"There's nothing mundane about any of you."

Even Noah and Audi closed their distance to gather around Michael with the others.

"Defenses are chosen when their abilities emerge as crucial to our cause," he said.

Sarah sniffed. "Abilities or coping mechanisms?"

Michael ignored her, adding, "Over the years, the concept of magic has devolved into everything from an ethical indictment to a new age joke, but by design it is available to everyone. Most of you were simply never taught how to access it."

"Daniel could have mentioned that," Drew folded his arms across his chest, "besides, weren't the Watchers punished for showing us how to use it?"

Michael's expression darkened. "Among many other things, they were punished for exposing you to the cruelest of its applications."

"Speaking of cruel," Laura slipped her hand into Bash's, "you ignored our summons, so why are you here now?"

"If I'd answered your summons, I could not have answered Andrew's prayer."

His smirk was not unlike one she'd seen Thomas make a dozen times and though irritating, she also found it strangely comforting to know that an archangel was not above the same level of obnoxiousness.

Drew let his arms fall to his sides and gaped at Michael in disbelief.

"Your voice is heard, my friend, but you're so much stronger than you realize." Michael squeezed his shoulder. "You don't always need what you think you do." Michael then turned and said, "Walk with me, Sebastian."

Side by side, they hiked away from the others until Bash fell out of step. He grew so tired that his legs would hardly move and then all of a sudden, they didn't. Michael let him collapse to the ground at his feet, gave the others a reassuring smile and then disappeared.

Laura screamed and ran to Bash, sliding onto her knees at his side. "Bash, Bash…wake up…please." When he would not, Noah and Audi joined her in the dirt with his medical bag.

They checked everything they could think of and then sat back on their heels. "His vitals are good, Laura," Noah said, "I think we just have to wait."

Chuck and Drew sat down on either side of her and Watson stretched out to rest his head on Bash's ribcage.

"Look!" Audi brought their attention to his forehead. A drawing emerged on Bash's skin in the form of what appeared to be a faint watermark outlined in red. He groaned as his eyes moved under their lids.

Drew examined the mark closely and said, "It's more of that angelic language."

"Take it easy, man," Chuck patted his arm, "we'll be right here 'till you get back."

In his dream, Bash was lying on a flat rock, soaking up the sun. His shirt was unbuttoned, and his arms were behind his head. He winked at Laura, who sat nearby and pulled his cowboy hat down to shield his face from the brightness. It occurred to him as she trailed her fingers lightly across his chest that it had been a long time since he'd felt so relaxed, and that made him nervous.

The sky darkened a bit, and he lifted his hat to see the sun disappear behind the clouds. An unexpected storm was rolling in and they would have to get going, but when he looked over to tell Laura, she wasn't there.

"Laura!" He sat up to scan the area, but she had vanished.

He jumped down and turned in a frantic circle until behind him he heard a familiar voice say, "Hey, now,"

He spun to see Richard jerk Laura by the hair and hold her to him with his forearm across her throat. To his left he heard another familiar sound that frequently haunted his dreams. Several goblins hissed as they advanced on Chuck, who crouched under a Palo Verde tree. The small machete Bash took from the Pinetop vampires lay on the ground just out of his reach.

Bash moved to get it for him, but the rattlesnake demon slithered over the rock and coiled up in front of him. Each time Bash took a step toward either Laura or Chuck, it struck at him, missing by only centimeters.

Drew approached from the distance, calling his name, but Bash waved him off, yelling, "Stay back!"

Then he noticed that Nick was with Drew, following in that monstrous hunch and dragging his clawed hands through the dirt. Bash pulled his pistol and shot the snake, but it reappeared, each time angrier than the last. He roared with aggravation, furious that he couldn't get to his friends.

Back in the real world, Laura did her best to soothe him as his body twitched and writhed on the ground.

Drew gave her hand a reassuring squeeze and said, "If he's answering my prayer, Michael won't let anything happen to him."

In the dream, Bash's heart was beating so hard that he could hear it and he thought he might go crazy with rage until Michael materialized at his side. He gestured toward Chuck and Laura. "They are your obsessive worries."

"They are people that I love," Bash growled.

"Out there, yes." Michael opened a small hole in the space in front of them so Bash could see himself lying in Laura's lap. Silent tears rolled down her cheeks and his friends looked on anxiously. "In here," he closed the window, "they get in your way."

"I am sick of cryptic, non-helpful statements and I swear to god if you don't just tell me what I need to know..."

Michael was amused, wondering what the man thought he could do about it, but tried to clarify himself anyway. "You can't access your messages if you're busy trying to help your friends."

Bash blinked at him. "Messages?"

"You have navigated so many treacherous crossroads in your life that you've become skilled at finding your way through the in-between places."

"You mean I make everything harder than it needs to be."

"Yes," Michael laughed, "and sometimes those painful pathways, particularly the self-inflicted ones, open up gray spaces that are closed to most other people. You do battle in your dreams, but why refight the same wars over and over? There is so much more for you here if you're willing to filter out what doesn't belong."

Bash's refocused on Laura as she struggled against the troll. "She belongs in my dreams."

"Laura was born with magical powers but her most useful talent is focus. She couldn't move the fire if she couldn't control her intentions. There's even a part of her awareness that's always right here," Michael touched the shield bracelet around Bash's wrist, "keeping you safe. So, what is she doing over there?"

When Bash thought about it, nothing in that dreamscape felt quite right. Chuck and Laura would never stand by just waiting to be rescued, but he couldn't walk away from what was happening. He took in the entire scene, concentrating on each scenario one-by-one. Drew was still coming toward him with Nick, and something was, in fact, itching at the corners of his mind, telling him that's what the others were keeping him from.

He couldn't believe it, but he heard himself say to Laura, "You know what to do, baby."

Richard yowled as Laura bit down on his arm and flicked her fingernails, engulfing him in flames until he released her. In his peripheral vision, Chuck crawled to the machete and proceeded to hack his way through the goblins. Bash kicked the rattlesnake out of the way and

Drew finally arrived with Nick. He was grateful for Drew's presence. He would know exactly the right questions to ask Nick, but Bash definitely had some of his own.

"Why didn't Jaya just kill me herself at the waterfall?"

Nick's deformity made it difficult for him to speak, but he appeared to be willing. "She's waited so long for her moment," he croaked, "playing with you puts her back in control."

"Does she really think she can get revenge on God by killing all of those people?" Drew knew she wouldn't stop with her own, albeit small-scale, extinction flood and quickly thanked every deity he could think of that Laura and Sarah didn't share Fiona's outlook on life. Their grandmother would have gleefully joined forces with Jaya and then would have tried to kill her before the rain even stopped.

"She doesn't care who suffers anymore," Nick scratched at the dirt, "her mind is a broken thing."

Bash was growing agitated, so Drew got to the point. "How can we stop her with only two pieces of the spell?"

"The Deanes have all they need to finish it." Nick held one of his hands in front of his face and wailed at its twisted shape.

Bash knelt in front of him. "How can I help you?"

"There's only one way," Nick snarled and squatted on his haunches, ready to pounce.

Bash backed away and drew his pistol, knowing he had one shot left after the rattlesnake. "Don't do it."

Nick wailed again and leapt for him, leaving Bash no choice but to fire into his chest.

"God dammit!" As Nick fell dead in front of him, Bash turned to Michael in near hysterics. "That wasn't real. You better tell me that wasn't real!"

"You've received your message so you can wake up any time you want to."

He holstered his pistol and fell against Drew for support. "I can't...I can't do this."

Michael tipped his head, lightly touching their brows together, and as Bash's senses dulled for his return to his friends, he heard the angel say, "Magic is not a gift, Sebastian; you will pay for it every day with your life."

When Bash's eyes opened, Chuck and Drew barely had him on his feet before Laura threw her arms around him, almost knocking him down again with the force of her hug. "How do you feel?"

"I'm good, baby. Really...I'm good."

And he was, though toward the end of his meeting with Michael, the others had watched in astonishment as his hair turned completely gray.

They were unsure of how to tell him about it, but Audi solved the problem by blurting, "Damn, talk about a silver fox."

Sarah pursed her lips and said, "Audra, please," but Laura winked and led him to the side view mirror on the Jeep so he could see.

"She's not wrong."

He shied away from other mirrors for the rest of the day, but that night while Laura was in the bathroom getting ready for bed, he stood in front of their dresser and stared at himself for a long time. Michael's red mark had receded and though it was jarring, the gray hair didn't make him feel as old as it might have before.

He wasn't necessarily looking forward to receiving any more messages, but he no longer felt so powerless. The whole experience with Michael had energized him and when Laura came to bed, he intended to make sure that she too got her energy back. There were things they needed to talk about, but instead he pulled her into his arms and stroked her hair until she fell asleep.

In the backyard, Thomas appeared next to Michael, who was peering into their bedroom window.

"So now you think you can just drag me wherever you want?"

Without looking at him, Michael said, "You cannot possibly believe that you've been wandering free on your own recognizance." He looked from the coziness of the bedroom to the dark expanse of the desert. "They are not safe tonight."

"I'm no Guardian."

"No," Michael finally looked at him, "you are a Watcher...so watch them."

When Michael left, Thomas took a walk around, grumbling about being reduced to a security guard, but as he scrutinized the place, he had to admit that the cowboy had provided Laura with a solid little house.

Her new garden had taken off once the weather cooled and he sniffed at the herbs and flowers the way another father might inspect his daughter's report card. He dropped a sprig of rosemary in his shirt pocket and turned the corner to see Gaab hovering around the kitchen window.

He zapped the Messenger Imp with a shot of electricity and snarled, "Don't even think about it."

"Alright, Michael," Thomas laughed to himself as Gaab squealed and flew away, "that was fun."

Chapter Seventeen

"The full moon is only days away, man," Chuck took a sip of cold coffee from the travel mug in his center console, curled his lip and then finished it off.

"Yeah," Bash gave his empty mug a shake and then put it down, "but Jaya won't leave the Other Side before that so if we can deal with Gaab and his pals, we'll be okay. In the meantime, we've got to find Nick."

They were on their way back from an early call to the Mercer place. Connie had been skittish since Bob was sent away for kidnapping Audi and every couple of weeks, she reported something strange on her property. The deputies never found evidence of anything, but they dutifully checked it out for her and fixed whatever was broken around the house.

When they arrived, she offered them some coffee, but it was seven in the morning and they could smell the whiskey in her mug, so they declined. Connie was devoted to her family, and with Bob receiving psychiatric care and Jenny in college, she didn't quite know what to do with herself. At one time, the Mercers were fairly active in the church, but Connie was embarrassed by Bob's troubles and quit going.

When no one from the congregation followed up with her other than to get the latest gossip, she withdrew even further. It was well known that witches made Connie nervous, but Laura and Rhonda stopped by one night with a tater tot casserole to see how she was doing. Even though Bob was sent away because of Laura's niece, they talked with her for hours.

Laura told Bash later that she didn't believe Connie was sad at all about Bob being gone. "She's just afraid to be alone, so we're going to start taking up more of her time."

No one in Chuparosa could claim to know what mental stability felt like, but judging a situation worse than theirs gave certain types of people a confidence boost and those people had a lot of influence. In Bash's opinion, Pastor McClane was in a bad position, though he didn't try very hard to get out of it.

As Holly Schmidt was learning, McClane would not risk his power in the church defending women with criminals for husbands. Not when there were plenty of *good* families, with money and opinions, in the pews every week.

On their way out to Connie's house, Bash had put in a call to Ben Bradford hoping that since McClane was out of town, he might feel free of the politics involved and pay her a visit. In any case, they were particularly interested in that day's complaint because according to Billy, who was working dispatch, she swore she'd seen a wolfman.

"Hand to God Chuck, that's what she said. A wolfman."

Connie stood, hands on hips, in her expensively renovated kitchen and glared at them both.

"Don't look at me that way, Sherriff Ruiz. I am not crazy."

Her eyes were glassy from the liquor, but she was obviously afraid. They took her even more seriously when she said what she saw was hairy and that its arms dragged through the dirt. When they searched the place, they could tell that Nick had been sleeping in her garage, but he was long gone. They assured her of as much and then Bash changed the oil in her car while Chuck chopped up what remained of a mesquite tree that split during the last of the summer storms.

Ben finished up his visit around the same time they finished their chores and jogged out to meet them. The passenger side window on Chuck's ancient county pickup wouldn't go down so Bash opened the door to talk.

"Everything alright in there?"

"Her feelings were hurt, and she won't come back to our church," Ben shook his head at the coldness of the situation, "but she seemed interested when I reminded her of Drew's services at the Y."

Chuck nodded. "He's working in Glendale now but he's coming by later, so we'll give him a head's up."

One did not have to be Sherlock Holmes to figure out how Benjamin Bradford was feeling at any given time and, noting his particularly troubled look, Bash leaned forward, asking, "Are *you* alright?"

"Can I follow you guys to the station?" Ben looked back at the house. "We should talk about something Connie told me."

"Yep," Bash said, "but we're goin' to my place for

lunch and to make some plans, so follow us there — you know where I live…on Alta Vista Road?"

"Thanks." He nodded absently and climbed into his little blue Ford Ranger.

If Drew had been in town, Ben might have simply passed off the information to him. Instead, he found himself intrigued by a not so small part of his brain that was excited at the possibility of being part of their work.

When they walked in the door, Laura, Mena, Sarah, Audi, and Tina looked up from the kitchen table. They'd been so engrossed in their conversation that they hadn't heard the trucks in the driveway.

Bash rubbed his goatee. "What's all this?"

Unwilling to burden Ben with their problems just yet, Laura smiled and waved him off. "We were brainstorming. I hope you're here for lunch, Ben, because I made chicken chili."

Ben had seen less serious looks at a church council budget meeting, but for the time being it was none of his business, so he sniffed the air and said, "It smells delicious."

As an associate pastor, and a single one at that, he was accustomed to people bringing him food and to being invited into their homes. It was luck of the draw as to the culinary talents of his congregation, but his mouth had been watering since they arrived, and he couldn't wait to dive into Laura's chili.

"So, what did Connie have to say?"

Bash hung his cowboy hat on a specialty holder by the back door and Laura suppressed a smile. He'd mounted a similar hook by the front door and every time he left the house, he would go to the wrong hook, swear, and then fetch his hat from the other room. As far as she could tell, he didn't even realize he was doing it. It was just an adorable ritual that he'd become accustomed to, and she would never dream of making him self-conscious by bringing it up.

"I think your brother has been hiding out in the church," Ben said. He was aware of Nick's existence because, for their own safety, Drew always gave his true friends the facts. Everyone in town knew at least a little bit about everything that went on, and Ben could be trusted to either shut down the rumor mill or, if the situation called for it, to let the rumors run wild.

"Holly Schmidt was in the loft the other day because some teenagers drew pictures of Jesus on a dance floor and put them in the hymnals," he chuckled to himself, "anyway, while she was up there, she chased away something that was sleeping in the corner. At the time I thought it must have been an animal of some kind, but what she describes matches what Connie saw and your description of your brother."

Laura retrieved some bowls from the cabinet and gave them to Mena, who said, "I don't know whether to laugh harder at the dancing Jesus or at the mental image of Holly going off on a wolfman."

"Well, now she thinks we've got demons in the loft," Ben wrung his hands, "and she wants to call Pastor McClane back from vacation."

"I'm sorry, Ben." Bash handed him a spoon.

"Please don't be. I believe Nick was able to find some comfort up there until she ran him off. I'm just sorry I can't tell you where he is now."

"God, she's such a bitch." Audi said as she arranged sour cream, shredded cheese, and hot sauce on the counter.

Bash frowned, "For what it's worth, I don't think he's out to hurt anyone but me."

No one there took comfort in that statement and as they piled their chili with toppings, the Deanes began to think out loud.

"I could bind him to us Bash," Laura offered, "keeping him here in Chuparosa until we figure out how to help him."

"Yeah," Audi agreed, "because if we banish him, he'll be a threat to everyone he meets."

Ben eyed the empty stool next to Tina at the island. "May I join you?"

She nodded, emitting a small squeak that he assumed meant 'yes' in shy girl language but he kept a respectful distance just in case. The two ate in silence for a while, listening in as the others tried to work out a plan. It was one of those times when Tina found herself a bit in awe of Audi who, at a very young age, had literally earned her place at that magical table.

"I wish I were that brave."

Ben used a tortilla chip to scoop up the last bite in his bowl and went to the pot for seconds.

"She's brave and powerful," he agreed, "but she would be lost without you."

He was right, of course, but every now and then Tina forgot how much they all needed each other, and she was touched by how he zeroed in on the importance of her friendships. She smiled at him and the spontaneous warmth of it caught him off guard.

He stared at her stupidly for a second, holding the ladle midair, until Chuck said, "Sam might be able to help us. Tina, would you please hand me my phone?"

He nodded his thanks as he took it from her and

began to scroll through his contacts without looking up. "Every record I found on Nick is sealed – we can't even get a picture of what he used to look like."

"Warren isn't likely to have one on him either," Bash grumped.

Chuck left for the living room to make his call and returned with more bad news. "Sam's deep under cover in Phoenix, so I couldn't reach him. I talked to Seth Ryder though. Do you remember him?"

Bash chuckled, "The guy with a hard-on for that shapeshifter in Jerome?"

"That's the one. He can't help us with Nick, but he said the department thinks it's a ghoul that's been tearing apart those women outside of Mr. Lucky's, so we can find Sam there."

Mena shuddered. "I read about that in the news."

Bash had never encountered a ghoul in his travels, but he'd seen the aftermath of their grisly work and Mr. Lucky's was the perfect hunting ground for them.

During the eighties and nineties, it was one of the highlights of West Phoenix night life. The main level was a country bar with a bull riding arena outside, and the basement level catered to a rock and roll crowd. Ownership changed hands quite a few times and several nearby businesses didn't survive the recession, abandoning an already dodgy area to the most sinister elements — both human and not. The arena and restaurant had been closed for years, but what remained of the bar became popular with a non-selective older crowd that tended to look the other way when things got dangerous, which they always did.

"Well, Chuck," Bash ran a hand through his hair, cringing a little when he caught his reflection in the window, "when was the last time you went clubbing?"

Audi snorted. "You two could be robbing a bank and still look like cops. You'll blow Sam's cover in five seconds."

"I'll do it."

Laura had been to Mr. Lucky's dozens of times during its heyday. She fondly recalled leaning on the fence, holding a Coors Light and watching the bull riders. Afterward, she and Cara would look out for each other while they danced with all the wannabe cowboys to whatever live band was playing inside.

"No fucking way," Bash blurted out. When every woman in the room shot him the same look, he regretted his knee jerk reaction, but stood by the sentiment behind it.

Laura was well aware of that and prepared to negotiate. "In the nineties, while you were all safely tucked away in your marriages, Cara and I were fighting for our lives in the mosh pits and the clubs."

"Baby, that place is—"

"Then the three of us will go together," Mena pushed Sarah in front of her, "all we have to do is find Sam, tell him what we need and get out. Right?"

"Are you hearing this?" Bash was increasingly alarmed by Chuck's lack of outrage.

"If it's a club," Audi stuffed some shredded cheese in her mouth and mumbled, "Why don't you just let me and Tina go?"

Tina's eyes widened in horror and Ben instinctively patted her hand. He shook his head as if to say, "they will never agree to it", and he was correct.

"You, uh, don't have the right aesthetic for that place," Chuck stammered.

Audi searched the browser on her phone for Mr. Lucky's and was unimpressed. "From what I can tell, the place has no aesthetic these days."

"What the sheriff is trying not to say," Laura clarified, "is that you can't pull off the desperate, aging barfly look as well as we can."

Chuck thrummed his fingers on the table. "We'd be outside watching..."

"Seriously?" Bash gaped at him.

"I know man, but I have an idea."

Chapter Eighteen

"This is a terrible idea."

Insofar as he could, Drew stormed around their tiny motel room. They'd booked a cheap place on Grand Avenue to better handle the logistics of their operation, such as they were. In theory, they would wire up the women with the new surveillance equipment, and Chuck and Bash would watch the video feed from an app on their phones.

They could communicate with them from their positions behind the building while Drew and Audi kept an eye on the big picture from a monitor in the room. They might even be packing up to leave in less than an hour. Drew harbored no delusions that he would have been able to talk Sarah out of it, but wished he'd been there when the decision was made.

For her part, Sarah couldn't wait to get inside of Mr. Lucky's. Laura was right, she was married during college and since Rueben didn't take her anywhere, she'd never been in a bar other than Isaac's.

Audi marched out of a door in the back and flopped

on the bed. "Just so you know, the oversized cockroach in the bathroom is demanding tips."

Sarah frowned. "I thought that was a little bat."

"Good god." Laura scrunched her copper curls in the mirror, gave herself a final spritz of hair spray and turned around. "Alright guys, how do we look?"

Audi whistled. "Get it girls."

They wore off the shoulder tops and cowboy boots with Wranglers so tight that not one of them could draw a full breath. That in itself reminded Laura that she did not miss her twenties.

"Damn," Chuck admitted quietly to Bash and Drew, "fifty-year-old Mena is still finding new ways to turn me on."

Bash smirked and gave each woman a small square case. "These are made to look like regular earbuds connected with blue tooth to your phone, and that's how we'll keep in touch."

"Sarah, I'm putting the body camera on you," Chuck fastened what looked like a cheap watch around her wrist, "stick close to them so we can see what's going on."

"You don't think this is overkill?" Mena asked as she put in one of her earbuds and dropped the case into her purse.

"It would be if three women hadn't already been murdered this week." Chuck's expression sobered, "If it's a ghoul, it can appear human. Around this place, he probably looks like someone you'd find handsome. A hot guy taking an interest – until he gets you outside." He clicked the magazine in his pistol and racked the slide. "Alright, give us a ten-minute head start."

Laura summoned a ride share while the deputies

walked the three blocks to the bar, then she sent Bash a one-line text: `We got this.`

When they left, Audi put on her headphones and patted Drew on the shoulder. "Come on, this is the most exciting thing we've done since..." he looked over his reading glasses and she cut her sentence short, "well, it's been at least a week."

The sign on the wall outside the bar announced that it was ladies' night at 8pm every night and, to Mena's offence, the bouncer didn't bother carding them. She and Sarah weren't sure what Laura was doing when she held out the back of her hand, but they did the same. Once everyone received a red bucking bronco stamp, he opened the door to an assault on their senses by a techno version of Before He Cheats.

Laura wasn't a huge fan of country music but had been convinced early on that certain artists were feminist vigilantes using their song lyrics as daring confessions, and subsequently bought all their records in support of that cause. Even so, the music was much louder than she remembered and by the time they reached the bar, she knew it would be days before they could hear properly again.

"Do you see him?" Bash's voice in Laura's ear was comforting.

"Not yet." She leaned over to shout at the bartender, "Might as well get things started!" and ordered them each a shot of tequila.

"Mom, keep your wrist up so we can see."

Sarah rested her elbow on the bar and spun slowly on her stool. Her breathing remained shallow with excitement as she was taking in the experience as much as she was looking for Sam.

Mr. Lucky's was crowded for a weeknight, and it was dim and hard to see. Laura began to wonder if they'd wasted their time until, at last, she heard his booming voice and located Sam with another man seated at a high top near the dance floor.

"Found him."

Since they were on the opposite side of the place and nowhere near the ladies' room, she would have to be creative to get his attention. Fortunately, her mother's unintentional instruction on how *not* to act like a grown up included master's level demonstrations in causing a scene. She examined the others at the bar, searching for a potential victim.

Two women, about their age, nursing double pours of red wine were ogling a younger man seated at the end of the bar. He'd caught Mena's attention when they walked in, and she'd given her and Sarah a nudge. Laura was certainly not above cougar-like thoughts but the way that particular young man hunched scowling over his drink reminded her of Brian, and all she wanted to do was ask him if he'd had enough to eat for dinner.

Her plan was set in motion by two much older men at the bar before she had time to prep her friends. The moment she looked in their direction, those men decided that they'd been invited to join them.

"Head's up ladies," was all she could manage before feeling one of their hands on her back. He'd positioned himself between her and Sarah while his friend moved in between Sarah and Mena.

"Oh, great." Drew scowled at the monitor.

"Actually, this is perfect," Laura said.

"I know what you're thinking, baby. Just be careful," Bash kept his voice neutral, but his impulse was to barge in and beat the shit out of them.

"Do you want to know what I think would be perfect?" The man shouted in her ear.

"Not really," Laura replied.

His friend noticed Sarah's ear pod and lifted her chin with his thumb. "You waitin' on a call from your boyfriend?"

"Maybe." She gave Mena and the wine drinkers a bored look, and though they rolled their eyes in a show of solidarity, he didn't appear to notice.

He leaned in close, took her hand and began to massage it. "Well, I'm here and your boyfriend's not so what does that tell you?"

Mena circled around behind Sarah's stool and took his other hand. He grinned at his friend and said, "I could get into this."

She wrapped her fist around his middle finger and bent his wrist backward until he hollered out and jerked away. "Crazy bitch!"

The first man grabbed Laura by the arm and pulled her off the bar stool, growling, "Something wrong with your friend?"

Sarah hopped down and gave him a shove. "Hey!"

"Why don't you clowns take a knee?"

Everyone looked up to see Samuel hulking over them. He was as unbothered as ever, clearly confident in his ability to control the situation, but he did have a glint of curiosity in his eyes. The two men sulked off to a table far away from them and Samuel inspected Laura's arm for a bruise.

"You lost darlin'?"

"No," she said, and made a face at the purple splotch forming around her bicep, "but we could use a hand with something else."

He took her phone and made a show of wanting to hear something, so she dug the earbud case out of her purse and gave him the other one. He put it on and scrolled through her music app. "Hey Bash, how's it goin', buddy? You have my attention."

Mena and Sarah chatted with the other ladies and Laura ordered beers for everyone while Bash gave Sam the few details they had on Nick and Warren Scott.

In the motel room, Audi squeezed the back of Drew's neck. "Look who that is."

He squinted at where she was pointing on the screen and at a table for one in the corner, almost completely hidden in the shadows, sat Cara Marshall.

"What is she doing there?"

Audi remembered Cara saying that Adam was the better person of the two of them and thought she might be starting to understand what she meant. "Tell the others later if you want," she said, "but I think we should leave her alone for now."

Cara had no idea what her friends were up to, but after Adam's story from the basketball game, the man she assumed was Samuel had intervened. For the moment, she saw no reason to make her presence known to them.

Her target was the young man at the end of the bar. She'd followed him there from an even less savory place where he'd tried to assault a sex worker. That woman kept a Doberman with her though, and he'd narrowly escaped with his balls intact. Cara found him stewing at Mr. Lucky's and expected him to take his anger out on one of the wine drinkers. Whatever they were doing, she would have to hope that her friends left the bar before he did.

Sam continued his conversation with Bash, flashing each of the women a grin. "I assume you need this info yesterday or you wouldn't have sent in the A Team."

"I'd appreciate it," Bash said.

Sam took a card from a narrow leather sleeve and reached around Laura, using his whole hand to slide it into her back pocket. "Call me tomorrow at this number."

Bash kept his tone playful, but his jaw was tight. "I wish I had some popcorn while I watch her melt your dick off."

"No time for that." Sam knew what he was about to say would cross a line and he was glad that Chuck and Bash weren't physically in the room. "I'm going to turn this place upside down in a few minutes and since I have the A Team here, I'd like to cash in this favor right now."

Chuck punched the trash bin outside. "Dammit, Sam. No!"

Drew stood up, knocking his chair over behind him. "Oh god. The ghoul is the guy at the end of the bar."

"Keep your eyes on me ladies." Sam's instruction was unnecessary since sheer terror kept them from looking in the young man's direction.

Mena could think of nothing but the news article describing the condition in which the murdered women were found. "What do you need us to do?"

"Mena," Chuck groaned, "Jesus."

"I'll go find your boys outside and you lead him to us. And remember this, leave him alone once he's down because a second blow will bring him back."

"I'm gonna kill you for this," Bash snarled.

Sam laughed, "I'll put your name on the waiting list."

Laura smiled sweetly, removed his hand from her pocket and shook her head. Then Sam shrugged and headed back to his table where he pretended to complain about her to his friend.

Laura ordered a second round of shots and they closed ranks. When they overheard one of the wine drinkers decide she'd worked up the courage to speak to the young man, Laura knew it was time to take a chance. Before the wine drinker could untangle herself from her stool, Laura was leaning on her elbows at the end of the bar.

"Gin and tonic." The bartender placed the drink in front of him and gave Laura an encouraging nod.

"I never cared for gin," she said, looking at her fingernails.

He took a sip and looked her up and down. "I noticed you're a tequila girl."

"Tonight I am."

"Are you done playing with those losers? Do you want to go have some real fun?"

"I'm with my friends."

He looked them over and shrugged. "They can come too."

Though they'd probably saved their lives, Mena and Sarah felt guilty as they passed the wine drinkers, who shot them looks of betrayal and left in a huff.

"What's your name?" Sarah asked him.

He ignored her, put some cash on the bar and stood up to leave. "My car's parked in the back."

Behind the trash bin outside, Sam and his partner were practically sitting on Chuck and Bash.

"We've got to be sure he's the one before we run out, guns blazing."

If there had been a car in the back, the women would have passed out from the shock, but Mena couldn't help herself, asking, "You got one of those new, invisible cars?"

Without warning, he grabbed her around the waist and lapped his tongue up the side of her face, leaving a trail of slippery drool.

"Ugh," Sarah gagged and raised her hand to throw him against the wall with her mind.

"Witch," he hissed and fell to all fours, stretching his neck from side-to-side and revealing bony spikes that had been hidden behind his ears. Once back on his feet, he leaned forward with his hands on his knees, and his back rippled with a rounded hump that rose along his spine.

"Okay, I'm sure." Sam let go of Bash, and the four men sprinted around the building in time to see the ghoul grab Sarah by the throat. He flicked a zippo into a trash pile, lighting a barrier of fire between them.

"How fun." Laura swept her arms in front of her, pulling the fire wall to the side. The men drew their pistols, but the ghoul was using Sarah as a shield. He was focused on everyone in front of him and didn't see Mena swipe a burning pallet slat from the fire. She ran at him from behind, swung it like a baseball bat and buckled his knees.

He let go of Sarah's throat and Chuck lunged to catch her as she collapsed, gasping for air. "I'm getting tired of being choked," she complained, the early design of a more protective necklace forming in her mind.

The ghoul began to scream as Laura engulfed him

in the wall of flames. Fighting the urge to unload his pistol into the thing, Bash took one shot, hitting him in the forehead. Laura moved to snuff out the fire as the screaming stopped, but Sam stopped her.

"Let it burn."

When the ghoul was reduced to ashes, Sam stood between Chuck and Bash with his hands on their shoulders. "You sure you don't want to come back to work for me? Bring the A Team with?"

Bash surprised Sam with a left hook, knocking him off balance and into a pile of rubble near the back door. He held his hand out to Laura, who stepped over the Special Inspector and into his arms.

Sam sat up on his elbows, laughing and rubbing his jaw. "Call me tomorrow."

When everyone cleared the area, Cara perched on top of the garbage bin with her legs crossed daintily over the side. She hadn't known the guy was a ghoul and made a mental note to ask Adam if it would have been safe to drink its blood. She doubted it. Adam would be pissed that she'd gone hunting without him again, but he would be very interested in the story she had to tell.

Her friends had likely saved her life that night but, tapping a long fingernail against one her fangs, she contemplated the underlying problem. She was still hungry.

Chapter Nineteen

Drew tossed and turned in Sarah's bed that night, reminded of an article he'd read recently about how lack of sleep during middle age could lead to dementia. As far as he knew, he and his friends had plenty of other health factors in their favor to balance out the risk.

At the very least, he was sure that by regularly fighting monsters, their exercise levels far exceeded the national average for their age group. Then it occurred to him that they probably wouldn't live long enough for dementia to become an issue and he upset himself by finding that a comforting thought.

Afraid he would wake Sarah with his restlessness, he brushed her hair back, kissed her forehead, and slipped out of bed. It was one of those nights when she slept naked, and her body shivered as a chilly breeze wafted over her skin through the open window.

With Audi in the house, Drew rarely even walked around without a shirt, so he pulled a hoodie on with his sweatpants and tucked the covers around Sarah, adding a soft throw blanket plucked from a reading chair near the closet. He padded into the kitchen and silently cursed himself when the glass door screeched through its track. He'd meant to give it a spritz of WD-40 but completely forgot. *Is that how dementia starts?*

The back porch was hardly recognizable since Sarah and Audi moved in. Laura's wooden worktable had been replaced by a pub style bistro set, and where giant planters of herbs once took over the space, Sarah filled pots of all sizes with tomatoes, onions, and peppers. He settled into the egg-shaped chair swing he'd hung in the corner and closed his eyes. His breath fell into rhythm with the hoots of an owl perched on the mailbox out front and he gave in to his thoughts.

It was unsettling how he'd been less surprised that they had to fight a ghoul than he was when Michael answered his prayer for Bash. That uneasiness was, no doubt, the cause of his insomnia, but the overall tattered condition of his faith after decades of confusion and disappointment was the source of a deep sadness that had slowly crept up on him over the years — one that he could no longer ignore.

After a while, the back of his neck prickled with a new presence on the porch, but since it was familiar, he kept his eyes closed.

"This is the hour I always preferred." Daniel said, taking a seat near Drew on the low brick wall. "Even in my human lifetime, the daylight hours were too chaotic for me to think clearly."

They sat together in silence for a long time before Drew slowly opened his eyes. "I always thought it would be nice to have a day between the days. One I could use just for thinking things through."

"You will never have enough time to think through

everything that brings you outside in the middle of the night."

Drew caught something in his tone and leaned forward on his elbows, but Daniel shook off his concern and stood to stretch. He had never relaxed to such an extent in front of them before, and Drew wasn't sure if knowing that angels also got stiff joints on occasion should be cause for comfort or concern. *Could they ever really get to know him?*

"Doubt is not a sin, Andrew." Daniel returned to his seat and leaned against the pergola. "Blind faith is easy for those who choose it, assuming they allow themselves to be led in the right direction. But what about men like you? The contradictions are overwhelming, and you know the questions burning in your heart will never be answered. To maintain even the smallest amount of trust requires the sacrifice of nothing less than your peace of mind...forever."

Drew's eyes reddened, but he laughed. "Maybe we'll get a softer cloud in the end."

"No," Daniel said, "but you deserve to know that I understand you."

Drew's shoulders relaxed a bit and they sat listening to the night for a while until an unnatural sound joined the owl and the insects. Daniel put a finger to his lips and pointed to the tip of a tail that had dropped through the slats of the pergola above them. A slightly larger version of Gaab squatted on the roof clutching a jalapeno in both hands, spitting out the little white seeds after each bite.

Sarah woke to the scratching of the demon's claws on the roof and jumped out of bed, tying on her robe. She started to call for Drew, but a skeletal hand reached around her neck and pressed her mouth closed. The banshee was gone when she twisted to face it, but its soft wailing echoed in her mind from every room.

"Who is it for?" she demanded, stomping in the bathroom, "Tell me." During its last appearance, it had given her the impression that Drew was not in mortal danger and dread gripped her heart as she thought of Audi down the hall. Though Sarah hadn't heard the witch's knock, she pleaded silently that it be her if the banshee was calling for someone in the house.

Moonlight shone through the glass block window next to the bathtub, giving her reflection the appearance of a shimmer in the otherwise dark room. She covered her ears and squeezed her eyes shut, crying out, "Please...just tell me."

Suddenly the wailing ceased, and when she opened her eyes, the shadow of the banshee emerged behind her in the mirror. It reached for her and though her breath caught in her throat, she took its hand and allowed the creature to lead her from the room.

Outside, Drew picked up a shovel and poked at the demon through the slats of the pergola. "Hey!"

It dropped the pepper and swooped over them, hissing short bursts of fire from its beaklike mouth. As it passed him, Daniel grabbed it by the throat and threw it against the wall.

Careful to keep a safe distance, Drew snarled, "Tell Jaya we'll see her on the full moon, and she better leave us alone until then."

Daniel let go of its throat, but before flying away, the firebreather slashed its claws down the side of Drew's neck. Drew tossed the shovel in the air, grabbed it by the handle and swung it, smashing the demon against the stucco. It hung there for a second and then fell spread eagle onto its back.

He stabbed down with the shovel and when its head was separated from its body, the whole thing dissolved, leaving an acid like etching of its bony wings in the terra cotta tiles.

Drew looked over at a pile of cleaning supplies that Sarah had left on the porch and then at Daniel.

"It's going to take more than a Scrub Daddy to get rid of that stain, isn't it?"

"Is a Scrub Daddy made of crushed rubies coated in burnt sage?"

Drew picked up one of the stiff yellow sponges and laughed. "Not the ones she bought at Target." He looked at Daniel again with fresh anxiety in his eyes. "It made sense that Thomas could do it, but how is Jaya sending demons for us?"

"People fear what they call the devil," Daniel explained, "but there are far worse things in Hell, and Lucifer does humanity a service by keeping them locked up. As the earth heaves and the veil thins, his job will become more difficult."

Drew sighed. "You're saying we could end up with some very strange allies?"

"Indeed."

They didn't notice Sarah watching them from the window over the kitchen sink or the dark, gangly creature at her side, and she was the only one to hear it when the banshee dropped its jaw open wide to scream.

∗ ∗ ∗

Drew picked up Bash in the morning so he could finally

collect his truck from Arley's, and Chuck was in the driveway when they returned.

"I thought we'd give Sam a call and," Chuck motioned toward Mena's Corolla, "it turns out my wife is here, so two birds, man."

Once again, the women were huddled around the kitchen table when they walked in, though on that day it was Laura, Sarah, Mena, and Rhonda poring over an enormous book.

"It's a bridging spell," Rhonda was saying, "but Audi can't do it. You need someone with similar life experience, someone who is on your level."

Bash had ignored the secret meeting the first time because he expected Laura to share the details with him, but his patience was wearing thin with her unwillingness to elaborate on her own.

"What's a bridging spell?" he said in a voice a bit harder than he'd intended.

Laura sensed his irritation but hesitated, casting a glance at the other women.

"Don't try to protect me, baby. Just talk to me." Bash's anger dissolved into worry.

Rhonda stood and straightened his collar. "Calm down, Sebastian. We're doing research, not keeping secrets. The spell bridges witches together, building in strength as each section is completed."

"Is that what Jaya's trying to do?" Drew cast Sarah a glance and closed the book. There was no title on the cover, but it was decorated with dozens of petroglyphs — some of which he recognized from the desert behind their homes.

Bash reached around him and reopened it to the page they'd folded in. "This is dark stuff."

"Jaya's a dark bitch," Sarah snapped, "and we need to be in her head."

A knot formed in Chuck's belly as Mena sat quietly at the end of the table, unwilling to meet his eyes. It occurred to him then that the Deanes weren't trying to protect the men they loved. They were protecting her.

His phone rang, startling them all with a sudden break in the tension. "This call is from the number Sam gave us." He put it on speaker mode and rested his phone on the kitchen island. "Sam?"

"I got the info you wanted on Nick Scott, but..."

Bash stiffened, "Just tell us."

"Here goes," Sam took a deep breath, "In the early two thousands, Gloria worked for an insurance company and Warren was doing road construction. She had Nick a few months after they moved in together."

Bash furrowed his brows. "So, he's about Becky's age then."

"Right. But Warren took off when Nick was two and Gloria flaked out. The boy was in and out of foster care and then in and out of juvenile detention. He even did some time a couple years ago for possession and petty larceny. Lately he's been stealing copper wire from construction sites and selling it for meth."

"Christ, that could have just as easily been me back in the day." Bash made a face in disgust, "I guess Warren wasn't going to be happy until he finally ruined someone."

"Here's where it gets interesting: before he found his way to Chuparosa, Nick was living in The Zone and a, ahem, friend of his told me that a few weeks ago he said he saw some strange creatures. This friend witnessed him going off on something only he could see. He also started to change his appearance, growing his hair and nails. The friend assumed he was just tweaking, but his behavior became so erratic that a bunch of guys got together and kicked him out."

Chuck looked at Bash and said, "He must have tried to go home to his mother."

Bash swallowed hard. "Sam, does your office think Nick killed Gloria?"

"No," Sam assured him, "the timeline doesn't fit. I think he found her dead and ran off. But listen, the timeline that does fit…"

Bash completed his sentence, "…is Warren's."

He and Sam were not great friends, but they were as close as they could be after spending so much time together hunting so many horrible things. Sam liked to pretend he wasn't a compassionate man, but Bash's earlier statement had made him uncomfortable, and he felt compelled to address it.

"Pay attention to me, Bash. There's no way you could have ended up like that kid. No fucking way."

"It pains me to say it, Cowboy, but he's right. I've never seen anyone fight against himself so hard and still win." Watson paced in front of Laura as Thomas joined them in the kitchen. "Allow me to pile on to your woes…"

"Who is that?" Sam asked.

Thomas began poking through cabinets and said, "You do not want to know."

"I'm pretty sure I do want to know but go ahead."

"Did you bake cookies this week, Laura?" Thomas opened a tin he found on the counter and frowned. "Peanut butter is not my favorite."

"Peanut butter is Sebastian's favorite." Laura took

the tin from him and placed it in the middle of the table for everyone else.

"Anyway," Thomas took a bite of his cookie and glared at Bash, "in the cloud community you've got Watchers like me, Defenses like you," he slapped Chuck on the back, "and Authorities like Daniel. The Authorities patrol the material world to make sure humans don't get hurt by abominations."

"Like us," Sarah snarked.

"It's not all about you, darling. In this case I was referring to Nicholas. Young Nick fell through the cracks because apparently, Jaya's made a connection in Hell. It's a weak one but she was able to use those lesser demons to reach out to Nick in The Zone."

"A connection with who?" Drew raised his eyebrows. "Or what?"

"It doesn't really matter because anyone can make a deal with anything. It would be a bit awkward for me if I tried to go back there to start an investigation, wouldn't it?"

Bash ran a hand through his hair. "I don't want to hurt my brother, but I can't help him if I can't find him."

Drew silently cursed Holly Schmidt and said, "I checked with Ben this morning and Nick hasn't been back to the church."

"Remember when Beau told us his kids saw something scratching around the Devil's Mouth?" Bash took a cookie from the tin. "Let's check that out."

Sam had been furiously taking notes but stopped with his pen in the air. "Bash, some of those mines have been abandoned for a hundred years and they were death traps even when they were in use."

"Well, we have a friend who knows his way around

them."

Chuck took the phone off speaker. "Thanks for the information, man."

Every alarm bell in Sam's brain was ringing. "Hey, were we just talking to an ang—"

"We'll be in touch." Chuck ended the call and returned their attention to the matter they'd walked in on. "Tell me more about this bridging spell."

Thomas cocked his head at Laura but, for once, didn't add anything to the conversation. Laura didn't trust him and had never considered asking him for help before then, but he would be an excellent source of knowledge if he were willing tell her the truth.

Rhonda was giving Chuck the basics when Laura cut her off and said, "Thomas, how might someone make it rain?"

He took another cookie and said, "Go to the top of a mountain and have sex for three days on a pile of henbane."

Bash looked up from Rhonda's book and said, "I'm game."

Laura rolled her eyes. "Henbane is a deadly poison, Sebastian."

"Oh."

"Well," Thomas shrugged, "it works."

Watson growled low to get their attention and went to stand by the back door.

"What do you smell?" Thomas peeked through the blinds and grimaced. "The hits just keep coming today. Sorry, Cowboy, even I wouldn't do *this* to you."

Warren stood on the porch, shifting nervously from foot to foot when Bash pulled open the door.

"Did you find your brother?" He blurted.

"Why?" Everyone followed Bash outside and circled around the older man. "So you can frame him for Gloria's murder?"

"Wait just a minute," Warren took a step back and held his hands up defensively, "I didn't kill her."

"I never said you did, but if you've got something to say..."

"Look, Gloria called me after she learned what was happening to Nick. I went over and listened to her crazy story, but what was I supposed to do about it? I told her I would try to find him, she collapsed, and I left. That's it. I had nothing more to do with it until I came to see you."

"You left her there?"

"I called the paramedics as soon as I could."

"You bastard." Laura flicked her fingernails and pulled a fireball into her palm.

"You didn't do it," Bash seethed, "but you sure as hell are the one to blame."

"I suppose you're a perfect man. A perfect father. Does your daughter know you've shacked up with a witch?" He shot Laura a hateful look. "What's the girl's name? Rebecca? That's very sweet."

Bash drew his pistol, grabbed Warren by the shirt collar and shoved him against the wall. "Never speak her name again, do you understand me?"

Chuck held out his hand. "Take it easy, Bash."

Warren's breath came in gasps, but he didn't back down. "I never promised anybody anything. They just weren't strong like us, Sebastian."

Bash handed Chuck his gun and punched the wall next to Warren's head. Shaking with rage, he released his father and spit on the ground at his feet. In a low and dangerous voice, he said, "I get my strength from my mother."

Chapter Twenty

The ledge over the entrance to the mine cast a shadow large enough for Adam to take shelter out of the afternoon sun. His chest swelled with anticipation as dust clouds appeared in the distance, kicked up by Bash's truck tires.

"Here they come." He knelt to pet Carl, his one-eyed brindle Pitbull terrier, who had also seen the dust and was panting with excitement. Adam and Carl once lived as lonely drifters, and even though they'd been surrounded by danger since moving to Chuparosa, Adam hadn't felt more at home, or more alive, in a century.

His friends tried to convince him that they could wait until after sunset to venture into the mine but, for obvious reasons, the brighter the better and with only one day until the full moon, the danger increased with every second of delay. As it moved across the sky, the sunlight crept over the toe of his boot. It wouldn't burn through, but he took a step back out of habit.

He waved them down and when the truck pulled to

a stop, Bash and Laura, Watson, Drew, Sarah, and Audi piled out to meet him. They were joined by Thomas, who appeared in their midst with his hands on his hips.

"This looks nothing like the Devil's mouth," he complained, marching up to the entrance.

Originally, the mine was so called because the long, jagged rocks protruding from the sides of the mountain looked like horns. Later, it was because far too many lives were lost in search of what ended up being a rather insignificant amount of gold. The county left Chuparosa to deal with it and in 1935, the Sheriff hammered wooden planks across the entryway and erected a sign that simply said, "Danger!"

It was known to be haunted and conventional wisdom had it that even if the ghosts didn't, the general appearance of the place would cause folks to steer clear for their own safety. Adventurous teenagers could rarely be accused of wisdom, conventional or otherwise, and everyone who grew up in town could tell you about a time they went with friends to check out the Devil's Mouth.

There were plenty of horror stories about the mine, but amazingly no one had been killed there since it closed, and Bash didn't want anyone in his group to be first.

"Listen up," he said as they gathered around him, "when we get in there and find Nick, the women will bind him with their spell and then we'll take him home. Chuck and Sam are checking out a place to keep him safe until all this is over."

Adam had known plenty of witches in his time but had never seen a binding spell — not one that worked anyway — so anxiety melded with his anticipation. He gave Carl a look that said, "we'll see", and agreed to the plan.

Carl and Watson were acquainted via their humans' frequent social interactions, and they were bonded by their mutual desire to keep those humans safe. Neither dog relished the idea of the other's existence, but they sniffed out a greeting and stood by for instructions.

"This will draw the spirits out and then Adam can ask them where Nick is hiding."

Audi reached into her backpack and pulled out a thick wand made of lavender and peppermint. She lit the end and nearly everyone felt the tension in their shoulders ease as the soothing scent of the thick smoke circled over their heads.

Adam's shoulders didn't drop, but his throat began to close. Choking and coughing, he backed away from the group. Thomas was studying some graffiti on the doorway and without turning around, he said, "Vampires are allergic to peppermint."

"Shit, I'm sorry." Audi let the wand fall to the ground and stomped it out.

Bash frowned at Thomas. "You could have said something before."

"I know."

Adam wheezed, "It's alright," as the smoke dissipated and he was able to catch his breath, "the Knockers will help us find your brother."

"Why do I feel like our definitions of Knockers are wildly different?"

Adam chuckled at Bash's correct assessment, then flipped on his headlamp, pulled the slats from the doorway, and led them into the mine. "Knockers will warn you of a collapse or an explosion, and if you're not an asshole, they'll even tell you the best places to dig."

They blinked at him.

"It's true. A miner won't go back down after a warning from a Knocker. It used to drive the owners crazy."

Rotted wood beams jutted over their heads as they made their way through the graffiti-lined tunnel and even the lightest of their boots stirred up the path, polluting the air with dust particles. The natural light ran out after a half-mile or so along with the entertaining graffiti.

A few steps farther, the air chilled to the point at which they could see their breath. Several wisps of light sprang from the ground and Adam tensed as the spirits flittered in between the friends who stood waiting for his direction.

Everyone felt that something wasn't right, and the dogs were on high alert, but Adam and Thomas were the only ones who could see the ghosts of the old miners. One had several long shards of wood piercing his skull, giving him the appearance of a living, screaming Voodoo doll. Adam swallowed hard imagining a dozen scenarios from his past in which such an accident might have occurred.

It flew behind Laura and wound one of the shards through the bun in her hair, jerking her head and releasing her curls.

"Ouch!" She swatted around her back, but it was invisible to her.

Adam gave Thomas a warning look, "They're agitated."

Thomas guided Audi away from the wall where a second spirit waited with a loop of rope for her neck.

He muttered a warning and the ghost dissolved into the rocks, letting the rope hit the ground.

"We're not the first living things to find our way back here this week."

Laura dug another elastic out of her pocket and tied her hair in a ponytail. "We must be getting close."

"Let's keep moving," Bash said. His spine tingled with warning, but he motioned for Adam to press on.

Not long afterward the tunnel split into three directions. Gagging, they instinctively turned away from the passage on the left.

"Bats." Adam said.

The tunnel directly in front of them was blocked with piles of rubble from a previous collapse, but there were iron tracks leading down the one on the right.

"Ore cars roll to the chutes and the inner workings of the mine," he explained, "this could be the way to the main chamber, which would make an excellent hiding place."

Both Drew and Bash found themselves wishing they had more time to inspect the artifacts scattered throughout the tunnels. Rusted lanterns hung from hooks hammered into the walls and blasting caps littered the ground. At one point Drew crouched over a wooden box, swatted away an enormous spider, and pulled off the lid to reveal piles of crusty old dynamite.

"See those crystals?" Adam said, keeping his voice as calm as he could. He took Drew's arm and gently moved him away from the box. "Over the years, nitroglycerin leaches out of the sticks...and it will blow us all to Hell."

"So, leave things alone," Thomas scolded.

Though the women kept their focus on the

indignant spider, ready to sprint if it advanced on any of them, they were appropriately alarmed by the dynamite discussion. As the spider finally scuttled away, its furry legs sounded as if they were tap dancing across the tracks. The spider was big, but not *that* big and they shared some confused looks until the tapping started again.

"Listen!" Sarah snapped, "someone's here."

They all went silent and, again, an uneven, light tapping echoed through the tunnel. It was as if someone dropped a handful of nails down a flight of wooden stairs. Then small pebbles began raining down on Watson who flinched as they bounced between his ears.

"Oh, god," Bash looked up for signs of new instability in the ceiling, "is the tunnel collapsing?"

"No, but pay attention," Adam replied as he ran his hands across the wall looking for an opening, "they'll be small." He pulled several foil-wrapped packages from his backpack and lined them up on a plank of wood. "They eat hand pies, and I make pretty good ones...if I do say so myself."

"Hand pies?" Bash was fascinated. "Beef or chicken?"

"These are made with potato and cheese."

Bash made a face, so Adam clarified, "Because they're vegetarians."

"Are you fucking kidding me?"

What looked like a doll from her childhood flashed in Audi's peripheral vision. She blinked a few times and caught it again, announcing, "Um, I think I just saw Miner Ken."

Laura knelt over Watson and Bash used his body to shield them both as more pebbles fell from the ceiling.

Everyone experienced the same disorientating visions until all at once the tapping stopped and a deep, far away voice said, "You need not worry about your hound. He was bred to guard the gate at the seventh circle, but now he guards you, which is a situation he much prefers."

Another flash occurred just outside of their field of vision and a different, more urgent voice warned, "If you are not careful, you will wake the beast that sleeps here."

"We've come to take him home," Bash said. He turned his head in the direction of the flickering light, but the small helper disappeared as he did so.

"Dammit."

Adam gestured to two more passageways ahead of them where the tunnel appeared to split again. "Which way do we go?"

They covered their eyes as the light flashed brighter and a harsher voice said, "You go back the way you came!"

A deluge of heavier rocks pelted down on them, and Adam glanced nervously at the box of old dynamite. "We'll find him ourselves if we have to."

The falling rocks slowed to a stop and for a few seconds, silence filled the tunnel. Then the deep voice said, "He has been poisoned with dark magic. Use caution if you must face him, and head north as quietly as you can."

Adam knew better than to thank the Fae, so he nodded to no one in particular and said, "That's good information."

Watson gave himself a shake and a thought occurred to Laura as she picked the remaining pebbles from his fur. "Does he have a name we should be using?"

The doll-like creatures dimmed out of their peripheral vision, but one of the voices answered faintly, "He is fond of Watson."

As they made their way to the north tunnel, Drew narrowed his eyes at Thomas. "You could have told Laura those things about her dog."

"I could have," Thomas agreed, "but she never asked me."

Chapter Twenty-One

"This is the place." Thomas ran his hands over the angelic script that Nick had scrawled into the walls outside the main chamber of the mine. "He probably thinks he's protecting himself with these sigils, but Jaya didn't bother to teach him the nuances of the language."

"What does it say?" Drew moved to touch it, but Thomas caught his hand.

"It says 'beware the damned.'"

Laura felt a flash of fury on Nick's behalf. Jaya taught him just enough to confuse him, but there was no telling what sort of power came with understanding angelic language. Her mother made her believe that she wasn't worthy of education, so as they had come across those symbols, Laura never thought to ask how to read them. She was furious with herself for leaving the research up to Drew. She couldn't even read what was burned into her own skin, and she vowed then to make Thomas and Daniel teach her.

Dirty blankets, empty water bottles, and snack wrappers littered the elevator cage in the middle of the room and rusted metal poked out from every wall.

Audi sighed, "Everyone's updated their tetanus shots, right?"

Nick was nowhere in sight, so Bash called out to him, "I know what Jaya did to you, Nick. Come home with me — let me help you."

"Why would you help me now?" Nick's garbled voice echoed through the chamber, but they couldn't see him.

"Warren never told me I had a brother," Bash gritted his teeth, "he left us, too...I didn't even know he got remarried."

At the mention of his mother, Nick emitted a sharp, tortured cry but said nothing more.

Bash opened his mouth to call for him again, but Adam held a finger to his lips. A familiar, light tapping started low in the wall and traveled up to where Nick was perched between the elevator crank shaft and the beam supporting a wooden ledge above Audi.

Realizing he'd been found, Nick extended his legs and unseated the beam. Drew sprang for Audi, shoving her out of the way and she rolled onto her back. Reaching out with her power, she hurled the ledge against the far wall before it crashed onto him.

"Jesus, Nick!" Bash yelled. He hauled Drew to his feet and started up a decaying ladder that leaned against the elevator.

"Wait, Cowboy, I'll send him down." Thomas disappeared and reappeared next to Nick on the second level. "I really don't think it's worth it, but he's willing to risk everything for you, so why not give your big brother a chance?"

With a roar, Nick pushed a wooden toolbox

through the planks, and they dove in all directions to avoid the falling hammers and chisels. Unwilling to use his powers in such a flammable space, Thomas leapt for him instead, but Nick jumped away, grabbing hold of some rusted iron track to swing himself up to the third level. That section of track broke free under his weight and an ore car smashed through both upper levels before Bash could get out from under it.

Adam lunged in front of Bash with his hands overhead and caught the car, but he was slightly off balance and stumbled forward. Bash thought for sure they would both be crushed, but Adam bent his knees and, with all of his strength and a dramatic groan, shifted the weight of the car, fell backward, and pitched it behind them. They came close to hyperventilating with relief and Bash even caught himself thanking God.

"Bash," Laura held up the jar containing the binding spell, "enough of this nonsense."

"Agreed." Adam grumbled and threw his body against the elevator casing, jostling Nick down to the second level. Nick clambered onto the ladder, but the wood rungs broke one by one, and his clawed hands shredded with splinters as he slid to where they waited for him below.

He hit the ground in a defensive crouch and backed away as Laura and Sarah approached him. Nick glimpsed the spell jar and sprang at Laura, so Sarah raised her arms to throw him aside. He tossed something at her feet, and she flew backward over the ore car and against the wall, unconscious. Bash choked on the air, remembering that very scene from his dream in Drew's vehicle.

"Sarah!" Drew slid to his knees at her side and lifted

her head while Audi checked her pulse.

"Jaya," Laura seethed and picked up a soft green ball. It was woven together out of Mexican feather grass and filled with cactus thorns and broken pieces of mirror. "This is a witch's ball. She made it to reflect our magic back to us."

She rubbed her hands together and filled them with static electricity, but loud, rapid tapping cautioned her through the walls. "Careful..." Bash put a hand over hers and pointed to another box full of crusted-over dynamite.

She nodded, opened her spell jar and tossed it to Audi, who swung her arms and hurled the contents over Nick, raining them down on his head. He charged at her middle, shoving her into the wall and dragging his claws down her arms. She slammed her elbow between his shoulder blades, ripping out a handful of his hair as his knees buckled. He yowled in pain and bit down on her hip before Bash and Adam could pull him off of her.

Nick was as strong as any vampire and he flailed his body against them, throwing Bash face first into the dirt. Carl and Watson each latched onto one of his extremities as Adam tried to wrestle him into submission, but again he bared his sharp teeth and tore off the tip of Watson's ear. The German Shepherd loosened his grip and Nick kicked away from them, scrambling up the outside of the elevator shaft and throwing everything loose he could find down on top them.

"Bash look!"

Fresh cracks formed across the ceiling and the entire structure began to shake and crumble. On the third level, there were dug out places in the mountain that were letting beams of light from the setting sun get through.

"Adam, watch out!"

Adam hoisted himself up to the elevator fly wheel. "Go! Go now!" he yelled down as he climbed.

Thomas reached out and hauled Adam over the landing. "Cowboy!" he shouted, "Get them out of here!"

The dogs led the way, sprinting toward what were by then deafening knocks guiding them from within the walls. Laura and Bash carried Audi between them, and Drew threw a still bewildered Sarah's arm around his neck, half dragging her as the tunnel filled with debris.

"Don't look back," Bash hollered, "just follow the knocks."

The Knockers led them out the way they came and, noticing that the only thing left of the vegetable pies was a handful of crumbs, Drew whispered silent thanks for Adam's apparently excellent cooking skills.

They tumbled out of the mine and raced for the truck. Laura flung the back seat forward, grabbed two blankets and spread them in the back for Audi and Sarah. "I'll ride with them."

The dogs hopped in with her and Drew climbed next to Bash, who leaned over the steering wheel, scanning the top of the mountain for any sign of the others.

Adam banged on the driver's side door, startling them so badly that Bash decided it was time to get his prostate checked. He wore a ski mask and gloves, but the sun had blistered the skin around his eyes.

Bash's stomach turned with guilt. "Get in out of the sun."

Adam climbed in the back seat and slid open the rear window so everyone could hear him. "Nick made it to Highway 85," he rasped, "he must have been confused because he turned back and made zigzag patterns across the desert." He let his head fall onto the seat rest, "I lost both him and Thomas right outside of town."

"The spell is working," Sarah mumbled from the bed of the truck. Her ears had stopped ringing, and her vision was beginning to clear, so she sat up and took over to Laura, who was opening the first aid kit and pressing a fresh gauze pad into Audi's side.

"She's right, Bash," Laura said, "Nick is bound to us now."

Drew held up his phone, which was just then blowing up with text messages from Ben Bradford.

"He's back in the church."

To everyone's relief, Billy was able to track down Noah, who waited for them at the front door with his jaw clenched as Bash staggered toward him, dirty and bleeding, carrying Audi in his arms.

Once they were settled, Thomas caught Laura pacing in the backyard and 'what iffing' the tunnel collapse. It was times like those that she wished she were a smoker so she had something to do with the nervous energy buildup.

She'd only ever loosely subscribed to the witch's notion of 'harm none' and had abandoned it altogether after meeting Thomas and Daniel. She would sort out her own safety on a case-by-case basis but would never hesitate to put down anyone or anything for someone she loved. Therefore, Nick presented her with a problem. Bash wanted to save his brother, but if she were forced to choose, Nick could die and she didn't care if Bash ever forgave her, as long as he survived.

Sensing her internal struggle, Thomas felt it was time to rip open a topic both of his daughters would eventually be forced to consider. "Have you prepared yourself for the possibility that even if he remains healthy, you will most likely live much longer than the cowboy?"

Laura wasn't angered by the question, somehow knowing that in his way, Thomas thought he was being helpful. "No, because I know that I won't."

Thomas did not like the sad, eerie smile she gave him. "Well, let's put a pin in that for now, my dear, because I have an errand to run."

She was furious. "You're leaving us?"

"You're mad now, but you'll get over it."

Adam nearly ran Thomas over as he sped up to the house, and then came close to colliding with Mena's Corolla as she screeched into the driveway at the same time. She and her daughter raced inside to check on their friends without saying hello.

He was grateful to have a few minutes of peace so his body could heal. After some deep breaths, the pain receded, and the skin tightened around his eyes.

"That's a neat trick." Thomas poked his head in the window of the pickup and looked Adam up and down. "It may surprise you to learn that I haven't met many vampires."

That was indeed a surprise, considering how much time Thomas had spent in Hell.

"You don't fit any of the stereotypes and, honestly,

it's disappointing. If you're not going to be a monstrous predator, you could at least be brooding and broken," Thomas made air quotes with his fingers, "the tortured soul thing."

Adam's lips thinned. "I have my moments." He sat up straight as Thomas turned to leave. "Where are you going?"

Thomas didn't answer and smiled to himself as he disappeared in a flash of blue light. He could not heal his body like a vampire, an unforgiveable oversight in his opinion, but the use of lavish theatrics had gotten him out of needing to a least a hundred times.

Adam slammed the door of his pickup as Bash and Drew came outside with Noah on their heels. The young paramedic had dressed Audi's wounds and was unsuccessfully trying to do the same for Bash.

"Sheriff, please."

Blood ran from Bash's elbow forming a red crust in the creases of his wrist.

"Fine," he said, resting his arm on the rim of the truck bed and wincing as Noah sprayed it with antiseptic. "We're going to meet Ben at the church," looking up at the brightness of the full moon, "and Jaya won't be far away."

Adam nodded. "I'm right behind you."

"She'll get in your head if you're not careful," Bash warned. The look on his face made Adam wonder just what she'd done to him, but there was no time for questions like that.

When Noah finished with the bandage, Bash looked down and chuckled. "That ore car would have flattened me for sure. I've got no way to thank you for something like that, but I guess now we're even."

Adam thought back to their battle with the troll and the horrific way in which he would have died if not for Bash's gift of blood and shook his head. "Let's not go back and forth like this, okay?"

Chapter Twenty-Two

Noah decided to check on Audi one more time before following the others to the church and her and Tina's conversation abruptly came to a stop when he opened the door. He'd been the topic and could not imagine which way it had gone for him, so he took a deep breath and joined them on the couch.

"If you don't want to see me, don't look," he poked at the bandage on her hip, "but I have to make sure this doesn't get infected."

Tina retreated to the kitchen and Audi took Noah's hand. "I want to see you."

When they touched, her eyesight clouded, and a fuzzy image of Drew stood beside the couch. *Annoying old man.* She shook it off and gave his hand a squeeze.

Noah's heart filled with hope, but he didn't want to give her the wrong idea. "I'm going to the church with them, and wherever else they need me."

Audi lowered her eyes. "I know."

It vexed her that she ended up making the same mistake as her cousin and Sheriff Scott who, aside from her father, were two of the most emotionally clueless men she knew. They had each pushed love away out of fear but if she were lucky like them, it would bounce back to her stronger than ever. There was only one way to find out.

She met Noah's eyes and said, "I was wrong...and I miss you."

With a wide grin, his cool exterior dissolved and he pulled her to him, rocking her in his arms. From the kitchen, Tina clapped her hands and then whirled away in embarrassment when they looked up and laughed.

"What now?" he asked.

"Go to them," she kissed him lightly, "and then come back to me."

When the door shut behind him, Audi laid down on the couch and closed her eyes. Right away a vision appeared of the hospital where she'd been doing clinical training, but something wasn't right. She wasn't the nurse, and Drew was there again, only his back was to her.

He smiled up at someone she couldn't see and then turned around and beamed at her, saying, "Do you think she'll call me Papa Drew?"

Audi sat up straight, yelping from the pain in her side and feeling as though her heart would beat right out of her chest. Drew held a baby in his arms. It was her baby, and she knew it in her bones — hers and Noah's. Drew was not the father in her earlier visions, he was the grandfather. She searched the vision desperately for Noah, then a knot of terror formed in the pit of her stomach.

Tina ran to assist as she lurched off the couch and hobbled into the kitchen. "Did your mom leave her car keys here?"

Laura's keys hung from a small hook by the door, but Audi wasn't sure she could control the Jeep in her condition. She took the key chain Tina dug from her mother's purse and weaved her way across the house.

"I have to go to them."

Tina was unaware of her best friend's vision, but she would have been shocked if Audi had stayed home that night. She smiled, remembering what Ben said about them being support staff and snatched the keys back from her. "You're not driving yourself."

Audi stared her down. "It will be scary, Tina."

She marched out the door, appearing much stronger than she felt and said, "Then I guess I'll be scared."

Ben Bradford and Holly Schmidt ran down the steps of the church to meet Bash.

"Nick's in the loft," Ben sputtered, "but he's not alone."

Holly's face looked like she just sucked on a lemon. "You didn't tell me the Sheriff was bringing the witches."

Nick had burst through the office window as she worked on Sunday's program, and she'd been near hysterics ever since.

"Go home, Holly" Bash ordered, "it's not safe for you here."

"There are demons in my church!" she shrieked. "How could demons just waltz into a church?"

She repeated some version of that question over and over until Daniel appeared in their midst. Her hands flew to her mouth in shock, and she backed away from him. "Another one!"

"Your church wasn't protected by the intentions of its congregation," he said harshly. "If you like, I'm sure the Deanes would be happy to help you with such things in the future." His voice softened as he turned to the others. "Nick's mind is almost gone, Sebastian, he's acting purely on instinct, and he's terrified."

"That poor boy came here looking for help, you miserable bitch," Mena chastised. She pushed past Holly, followed by Sarah, who, for effect, used her power to fling open the double doors.

Ben ran up the steps after them. "You won't get by those demons."

"Yeah, they will." Bash racked the slide on his shotgun and pressed ahead.

"Oh, great." Drew looked up to check the position of the full moon and caught a glimpse of several goblins cresting the hills behind the church. "Jaya's pulling out all the stops tonight."

Adam bared his fangs and said, "That's easily handled." Since being staked by one, hunting goblins was one of his new favorite hobbies.

"Would you mind?"

"Not at all." Adam's mouth formed a sinister smile and then he whistled for Carl. The two of them set out for the hills and Drew heard the squeals of dying goblins as soon as they disappeared into the darkness.

Drew took the steps two at a time to catch up with the others, then gaped in horror, completely unprepared for what waited inside. A dozen or more imps of all sizes circled close to the ceiling, occasionally diving low to blow flames at various targets. Small fires burned everywhere, and the smell of sulfur permeated the smoky air. A demon crouched on the pulpit, spinning a cross like a top and a larger one sitting on the back of a pew ripped pages from a hymnal and crumpled them in piles for the imps to ignite.

Drew closed his fist on the cross around his neck and then drew his pistol. "Ben, you should go."

Ben shook his head. "You're going to need more than weapons to win this battle."

* * *

Brian and Becky were making out on her couch when Thomas appeared in the living room. "Tsk, tsk."

"Jesus Christ!" Brian jumped up and pulled a blanket over her.

"No, Brian, it's Thomas. Remember?"

"What," Brian gritted his teeth, "do you want?"

Thomas opened the refrigerator and helped himself to a small box of chocolate milk, pleased that Becky's kitchen had a supply of tasty snacks. "There's a nasty ruckus in Chuparosa right now. Your parents would be happy to keep you out of the fray, but I'm convinced that the family that faces mortal danger together..."

"Does what?"

"Well, probably dies together, but your elders have a better chance of not doing that with your powers on hand."

"I should have known." Laura had kept Brian up to date on the Jaya situation but somehow made it sound like a much smaller problem than it was.

Becky bent to put on her shoes and said, "It will take hours, and it's supposed to snow, so we better start driving now."

"I know a much faster way," Thomas unfurled his wings, "and besides, you're not going."

She crossed her arms. "Oh, yes I am."

"Assuming you survive the trip," Thomas sighed, "be sure to tell the cowboy that this was your idea."

As three of them landed in the church sanctuary Becky fell to her knees to throw up.

"I warned you."

Thomas scanned the hazy room in time to see Daniel swipe the cross from the demon on the pulpit and plunge it into its forehead. He curled his lip when it howled and thrashed, dissolving into a putrid sludge that soaked into the rug.

The imps near the ceiling squawked with rage as Drew fired his 9mm at the porcelain baptismal pool. When it shattered, gallons of water flowed down the aisle, putting out many of the little fires and restoring a good portion of his mental health.

"See?" Thomas looked from Brian to Becky and said, "We almost missed all the fun." Then he cupped his hands to his mouth and yelled, "It's ten o'clock, do you know where your children are?"

Bash glared over his shoulder. "Dammit Thomas!"

"You'll never guess what I caught them doing."

"Cover us!" Laura shouted as Watson followed her, Sarah, and Mena up the stairs to the loft.

Brian gave Bash a guilty look and fired a stream of electricity out of his hands to scatter the imps above them. "You can kill me later."

Bash raised the shotgun to his shoulder, "If you two make me a grandpa I'll let it slide."

It was Brian's mouth that fell open that time, giving Bash another reason to smile as he blasted the demon off the back of the pew.

Upstairs, Nick cowered in the corner of the loft with one hand over his head and the other slashing wildly at the air in front of him as one of the demons flicked at his ears.

"Hey!" Mena yelled, "Try that shit with me!"

She gulped as it turned to her slowly and whispered, "Okaaaay...Meeeena."

Watson rushed to her side, barking wildly. His mangled ear still bled a bit from where Noah stitched it up, giving him an even fiercer look, but the demon advanced on them anyway.

"Traaaaitorous hound...your laaaast day has come."

"I don't think so." Laura flicked her fingernails and filled her hands with fire. It puffed out its chest and filled its own palms with fire, so she gave it a sweet smile, adding, "I'll even let you go first."

Nick began to writhe on the floor behind the demon and Sarah said, "We don't have time for this."

Laura gave the demon a shrug, snuffed her fire and wrapped it in a net of static electricity. Then, Sarah raised her arm and sent its electrocuted body twitching into the belfry.

"Nicholas," Mena cooed, "we're here to help you."

He flopped onto his back and Sarah used her power to hold him still while Laura knelt beside him. His eyes were wild, and her heart went out to him, but she pushed one hand down on his forehead and held his nose with the other.

When he opened his mouth, Mena emptied an entire vial of an amped up version of Laura's most powerful sedative down his throat. The three of them focused their intention on his well-being as he choked it down and in moments, his eyes closed.

"We don't know how long this will last," Sarah whipped the braided ropes away from the drapes, "so roll him over." While they tied him up, an imp flew by and lit the drapes on fire. The flames traveled down the thick velvet and into the rug, surrounding them and blocking the stairs. Laura could hold it back, but they wouldn't be able to get Nick out, so she leaned over the banister and shouted, "Sebastian, I need you!"

He responded to those particular words as if they'd been coded into his central nervous system and killed the imps in his way with robotic efficiency as he bounded up the stairs. Laura pushed down the flames along the landing when Bash reached the top, and he called for Drew to help them drag his brother outside.

"Ben, I have to go," Drew said, "you need to get out of here."

Ben started to say something, but the whoop of helicopter blades drowned him out and Samuel's unmistakable voice thundered from a loudspeaker, "Sebastian Scott...get your people on the roof!"

Chapter Twenty-Three

Outside, Thomas and Daniel found Gaab peering through the stained-glass windows. Thomas grabbed his footless stump and shook him until his jaw went slack. "Messenger, you will tell me everything I want to know."

Lately, Gaab feared the angels more than he feared Jaya, whose behavior was increasingly erratic. He doubted she would even remember him and didn't wait for Thomas to ask any questions before blurting, "She has made many deals to build her army and sinks further into madness by the day. She cannot flood the entire west if the Deane witches won't help her work the spell, but with her thirst for vengeance she'll destroy Chuparosa instead."

"Where is she now?"

"She's preparing for them atop the butte."

Daniel said, "I'm going," and disappeared before Thomas could argue.

Thomas used his elbow to break the window and stuffed Gaab inside. "Get those kids out of there."

Knowing the Sheriff and the witches had lost patience with him, Gaab flew directly past them and buzzed over Watson's head, shouting, "The young ones will be trapped."

Watson's ears perked up and he nudged at Laura's hip, but she was holding back the ever-growing fire, so he ran and barked at Bash who was helping Mena on to the window ledge.

"Find Brian and get out of here, buddy," Bash pointed toward the front of the church and followed up with Watson's favorite trigger word, "outside, outside!"

If a dog could roll his eyes, he would have but Watson jumped through the fire and followed Gaab down the stairs. He charged into Brian's knees nearly knocking him over and then bit down on Becky's jeans to drag her away.

"Okay, okay we're going."

Brian threw a net of static electricity, singing Gaab's tail and taking out a majority of the imps who remained near the ceiling before ducking through the side door with Becky and Watson.

Out front, Noah almost forgot to put his truck in park before running into the burning church. He hadn't seen Brian or Becky and assumed that everyone was trapped, but inside, the eerie smoke-filled place seemed deserted and he almost left before catching a glimpse of Ben at the altar.

"Pastor Bradford!" he yelled, "you can pray later, let's go!"

Noah's stomach turned when Ben remained still. Staying low, he ran to the altar and found that Ben was conscious but bleeding heavily from a cut over his eye. He knelt, put Ben's arm around his neck, and heaved them both to standing. As they started for the doors, the pastor froze.

"They're back!"

Noah craned his neck around to see two lizard demons as big as Watson lumbering toward them with three imps hovering overhead. He sat Ben down and drew his pistol from a holster on his backpack, killing one of the lizards with a shot between the eyes. The imps made sure he wouldn't be that lucky again by flying at his face and lighting his backpack on fire. He fired everything he had but only took out two of them. The remaining imp dragged the burning backpack away and Noah could not get to his extra magazine.

He looked at Ben and asked, "Where's your gun?"

"I'm sorry," Ben could sense an oncoming crisis of faith and suddenly related to Andrew more than he ever wanted to, "the only weapon I've ever needed until now is prayer."

Noah let his head fall back with the realization that he was fighting demons with the only pacifist in Chuparosa. "Well, then you fire off those prayers, and fast."

Brian and Becky ran to the front of the church to get a better look at the helicopter. "Why do I think we've missed a million details about your Uncle Nick since our parents left Flagstaff?"

"Isn't that Mena's car?"

They guided the Corolla to a safer place in the dirt parking lot and helped Audi from the passenger seat.

"What happened to you?"

Audi was pale and wide-eyed, crying for Noah as she leaned against the car.

"I haven't seen him." Brian scanned the area and

caught sight of Noah's pickup, "He wasn't inside, was he?"

"And Ben?" Tina's normally soft voice was shrill with worry for her friends.

"Shit." Brian stared for a second at the flames leaping from the broken windows and then sprinted toward the doors, followed closely by everyone but Audi limping behind. They passed Gaab on the way, who wheeled around in the air to follow them, afraid of what Thomas would do to him if they were to die.

The smoke was much thicker by then and when Watson ran ahead, they lost sight of him right away.

"Get down low!" Brian shouted.

Three pews in, they heard Watson's bark and followed the sound to the altar. Noah had emptied the flowers from a tall metal vase and was swinging it at the demons. Knowing his lungs were giving out and that he was nearly blind from the smoke, the imp toyed with him, zooming in and out of his reach.

It didn't notice Brian shoot a stream of electricity and cried out in confusion as he dragged it into Noah's strike zone. When the vase connected, the imp smashed into a cross hanging over the piano where it sizzled and dissolved on impact.

Watson latched his jaws on to the hind end of the giant lizard which lashed its tail in annoyance, inadvertently flinging the dog into a much better position near its head. He sprang forward and sank his teeth into the demon's neck so deep that Adam would have been impressed. Becky pulled Watson away when the lizard fell over, and Brian electrocuted it just as Noah toppled into their arms.

Tina steadied Ben against her body and depression

set in on him as the foyer suddenly seemed miles away. He looked up to whisper a prayer for them right when the flames ate through the supports of an immense wooden beam. He didn't have time to warn everyone before it fell.

He squeezed his eyes shut and waited for the impact, but it never came. When he blinked, the beam hung overhead, and Audi stood in the archway holding her shaky hands out in front of her. With the last of her strength, she used her power to throw it across the room and then crumpled to the floor.

Gaab took her by the shoulders and furiously flapped his wings to drag her out the doors. Figuring bruises were better than burns, he let gravity take control on the steps and left her in the dirt so he could guide the others out. They were maddeningly slow, and Gaab could not understand why they didn't just leave the broken humans behind, but eventually everyone staggered out to the landing as a huge chunk of the ceiling fell down behind them.

In the loft, Bash hoisted Nick's body out of the window, then Laura released the flames and Drew helped them both onto the roof. "Damn," he straightened up and took his first real look at all the damage, "It's a good thing we told everyone to get out."

Sam flew the helicopter as close to the roof as he dared and, secured with a cable, Chuck leaned far outside the doors to lift Mena and Sarah inside. Drew climbed up next to help hoist Nick, then Chuck clipped him to his own cable so he could load Bash and Laura while Chuck shackled Nick to the side.

Drew pulled Laura up, but Bash wasn't there when he turned back around. A gangly demon had followed them out and it had Bash by the throat.

The banshee began to wail low at Sarah and she put her hands over her ears, begging, "Not now...please."

Drew grabbed hold of Laura's waist as she leaned out and shot a fireball into the demon, who released Bash long enough that he could make the jump. As soon as he grabbed the skids, Sam flew away and Laura shot a bolt of electricity into the demon, knocking it off the roof and turning it into a smoldering patch in the dirt.

Once inside, Bash scrambled to the back, yelling, "You could have given me thirty seconds!"

Sam laughed, "You're just lucky we eavesdrop on all emergency calls."

"And that Billy made one," Chuck added.

Early on, Billy set their fancy new radios so that he could listen in and had been keeping an ear on them since they first met with Jaya.

Sam gestured to an odd-looking storm brewing over Shock Butte. "What do you suppose is going on there?"

They spied Daniel and Adira positioned near the edge and Jaya lurking on the far side as Sam flew them closer to the butte.

Bash yelled, "Drop us there!"

"That's a lot of lightning," Sam warned.

"Just get us as close as you can."

Chuck's voice cracked with emotion as he pulled Mena close. "Promise you'll come back to me."

She said, "I promise," with such conviction that he didn't doubt her. Then she kissed him and jumped before he could see the terror in her eyes.

Bash was the last one out, shouting to Sam, "Where are you taking Nick?"

Chuck gave him an assuring nod. "It's okay, man!" he called out and they flew away.

The clouds moved across the sky with unnatural speed, intermittently blocking the light of the full moon and every plant on the butte vibrated with Jaya's power.

"You can feel the crazy in the air," Bash grumbled.

"She's working the spell by herself to destroy Chuparosa," Daniel explained.

Adira's voice filled their heads. "She will tell you that her army waits on the Other Side, but no one there will follow her."

"Her friend group is dwindling," Laura pulled out a pocketknife and bent to cut a strand of desert grass that wound itself around her ankle, "but we have to watch out for everything."

"Jaya!" she shouted, "you still have time to stop this!"

A sprinkling of raindrops fell on them briefly and then the rain moved near Jaya. She waved her hands and forced the clouds over a natural granite tank that drained off the side of Shock Butte and into town. The tank was occasionally the source of flash flooding and would be an excellent funnel for her method of destruction.

"That's not good." Drew said to himself, gazing down at the lights on his street.

"Sarah, look out!" Mena cried as one of the surrounding Saguaros swung its arm, narrowly missing her.

"Have it your way." Laura filled her hands with flames and threw a fireball at the Saguaro, vowing silently to plant another of the protected species the second she could.

Jaya shrieked and scratched her fingernails down the sides of her face, smearing the blood running from the gashes on to her arms as if completing a warpaint ritual. Then her demeanor abruptly changed, and she smiled sweetly at the men.

Drew fell to his knees in front of her and Bash lifted him up urging, "Just push her out of your head."

"Oh, Sebastian," she purred, "I'm just trying to have a little fun."

She snapped her fingers and an Occotillo near the edge began to twitch. It's pole-like branches reached out for Bash, wrapping thick spines around his legs and dragging him off his feet.

"Leave him alone," Drew snapped.

It occurred to him that he could take her right there and he imagined the two of them, naked and writhing in the rain. Maybe if he felt good enough to her, if he held her tight enough, she would end the madness. He covered his ears and shook his head trying to force the images out of his mind.

She grabbed his throat and squeezed. "You know you like this."

He did. His body quivered for her but while she could pull on his impulses, he would not let her control his will to act on them. Her grip was like iron, but he used both hands to jerk on her arm, bending her elbow and pulling her forward. He butted her head with his, and though he saw stars for several seconds, she released him and stumbled back.

He was wobbly but he advanced on her, growling, "I'm ready if you want to fight."

"I changed my mind," she said haughtily, "and I wish to speak to my sisters alone."

She snapped her fingers again and the Ocotillo dug into his torso.

"Jaya, stop!" Laura demanded, but in one swift movement Bash and Drew were pulled over the side.

Chapter Twenty-Four

Drew felt his wrist crack from the impact. They'd fallen down to a narrow ledge on the side of the butte. Blood soaked through the knees of his pants, but he was fairly sure there were no other broken bones.

The ledge was almost twelve feet from where the Ocotillo grabbed them and luckily Bash landed right beside him, though his head bounced off the ground when he did.

Drew crawled to his motionless body and then called up to Laura, "He's alive!"

"You bitch." Sarah turned on Jaya and threw her against a barrel cactus.

Jaya sprang up and flailed her arms wildly, stopping only to pick out a couple of thorns.

"You think you know loss?" she screeched, "Everything was stolen from me!" She stomped around them, frantically tapping her temples with her fingers. "We could have been a family — we could have freed the Other Side, but you're too selfish!"

"You speak of family and freedom, but all you want

is revenge," Daniel said, "your mind is as damaged as poor Nick's."

Adira crouched long and low, stalking behind and ready to pounce. She silently closed the gap between them and pushed off her front paws, knocking Jaya to the ground. Relief washed over Laura who thought for sure Adira would be the one to kill her, but the mountain lion's body went still. When Jaya pushed her off, a crudely carved dagger protruded from her side.

"Just a little warning of things to come," she taunted.

The Bobs raced down from the rocks they'd been hiding in and licked at Adira's wounds, but she swiped at them weakly with her paws. "Fools...it's dipped in venom."

Laura's cries of outrage echoed down to Drew. He looked from Bash to the top of the ridge and swore. Bash let out a pained moan and Drew rested a hand on his forehead, whispering, "Stay alive...please." He then set his jaw and proceeded to climb, one-handed, back up the butte.

He called for Sarah near the top, but it was Daniel who helped him over the side. "Jaya is increasingly unstable, so wait here and provide cover." He peered over the edge and added, "Sebastian is safer where he is."

The rain over Jaya fell harder, matting her soaked hair to her face and diluting the blood smears, giving them the appearance of pink watercolors running all over her skin. The natural white tank filled quickly and would soon flood the town, making it too late to reverse the spell.

"We won't let you do this," Daniel said.

"You!" Jaya's face twisted with fury. "Your kind left me there to rot!"

"What you've become...you did to yourself."

With a crazed laugh, she pitched handful after handful of broken tumbleweed at him and then called out the hateful words that would adhere the spores.

"Stop!" Laura threw a bolt of fire at her, but Jaya pushed it into the clouds. They thundered in protest and released gallons more rain that then spilled over the tank. "Dammit!"

Daniel stumbled, dizzy and weak as the nitrates in the tumbleweed sank into his system and poisoned his organs. The banshee appeared between them wailing for Sarah's attention.

She stared blankly at it until the truth finally dawned on her and she shouted, "Daniel! No!"

Jaya twirled away kicking her bare feet through the puddles, singing, "Told you so...told you so..."

On the ledge below, the Bobs alternated between prodding at Bash's ribs and licking his face. At last, he began to stir as what felt like little strips of wet sandpaper swiped across his eyelids. He raised a hand to swat them away and then heard their small voices in his head.

"Help!"

"Help!"

"Hurry!"

"Hurry!"

His vision blurred and then cleared and then pain throbbed around his eyes, blurring them again. He covered them with his hands and the Bobs, fearing he would black out again, nipped at his ears.

"Climb."

"Climb."

Bash had never seen them so agitated. He rolled onto his side and pressed himself up, noticing right away how eerily quiet it was up top. A sick feeling crept through him, and he tried to yell for Laura, but what came out was little more than a loud cough.

"Okay," he told them, "but you've got to help me."

"Now."

"Now."

One of the bobcats nudged at his back while the other locked its teeth onto his shirt, helping him stand. He ached everywhere and the punctures in his skin from the Ocotillo thorns stung like fire, but he staggered to the cliff wall and slowly made the climb.

Once over the edge, he fell on his belly and his vision cleared to reveal his friends huddled over Daniel's body.

"Laura?"

Tears of relief flowed when she saw him, and she fell against him as he crawled to her side.

"The poison is moving too fast," she sobbed, "Sebastian, I can't stop it."

The contents of her magical medicine bag were strewn around her, but spasms ripped through Daniel's body and a combination of blood and foamy saliva dribbled from his mouth.

"Thomas!" she called out, hoping that somehow, he could hear her, "help us!"

"There's nothing I can do for him." Having arrived just moments before, Thomas had remained invisible, watching the scene play out.

Daniel lifted his head slightly. "Thomas," he panted, "do you hear it?"

"Hear what?" Thomas crouched beside him and pulled a handkerchief from his pocket to wipe Daniel's mouth.

"Do you hear Heaven's call?" Daniel closed his eyes, struggling for every word, "Will you answer it? Brother?"

Thomas sat back on his heels and took in the scene. His daughters were only meant to be an experiment. He once thought that he was merely breeding powerful minions who could help him escape his unbearable prison.

He expected nothing more than their aid and allegiance; but he would be lying if he said he wasn't proud of the smart, thoughtful women they turned out to be. It was annoying how they fought him, and their disrespect was intolerable, yet there were brief moments as he had grown closer to them when he knew in his heart that someday they would accept him as one of their own damaged Defenses. *Damaged, but not broken.*

He would always believe that his punishment was harsher than he deserved but he'd been consumed with bitter sadness for centuries and he was so tired of it. Daniel was right—there was a voice. It was a voice he never thought he'd hear again so for a year he'd stubbornly ignored the call.

Thin strands of lightning rose from the butte and curled around Daniel's convulsing limbs. He reached for Laura and touched the stone around her neck — the stone he'd given her the day they met. A surge of warmth flowed through her soul and then his hand fell across her lap as he died.

"Daniel?" She looked up at Thomas through her tears. "He's gone back to Heaven, right?"

Thomas shook his head. "Heaven is an angel's home, Laura. Not his reward." He placed Daniel's arm across his chest. "He served his purpose, and now he's gone."

"He can't just...die," Drew protested.

"We have many powers, but our bodies are no stronger than yours."

Adira nuzzled her head into Daniel's neck and Drew's shoulders shook with silent sobs. The banshee stayed close to Sarah, who stood rigid with grief, and placed a skeletal hand of support on her back. Bash buried his head in his hands. It was too much. Daniel's death was too much to ask of them after everything else.

Between his physical pain and the ache in his heart, Bash wasn't sure he could continue, but the Bobs bumped their noses against him, whimpering softly in his mind,

"Help."

"Help."

He went to Adira and ran his hand along her remarkably soft fur. Her breathing was labored and the wound from Jaya's dagger pulsed with black swelling. It looked like a rattlesnake bite, and he'd seen some bad ones, but he'd never seen venom so aggressive. There was no telling what Jaya had collected and he thought briefly of the snake demon Daniel killed in the forest before forcing it out of his mind.

"How do I help you?" His red eyes pleaded with her to give him some clues.

She could no longer speak so he picked up the vials from Laura's bag, reading the labels and tossing them aside until he found one that read, "charcoal," and another that read, "antivenom". He had no reason to believe that it would help her any more than it helped Daniel, but they were different creatures attacked with different spells and he had to try something. He tipped the vial into her mouth and then dribbled the charcoal over the wound, muttering his own profanity laced version of healing intentions.

"I don't know if this will work," he cautioned the Bobs but kept some hope in his heart.

Laura hiked the desert almost every day and came across any number of venomous creatures. Her antidotes would have surely rivaled anything on Noah's ambulance.

Content to wait and see, the bobcats stretched out next to her, and the entire group clustered near the poisoned bodies deciding what to do next while Jaya chanted and danced seductively around the rain that somehow fell only into the white granite tanks.

Then Sarah noticed something different about the lightning. The strands grew thicker and crackled with static. "Look at that." She forced some of it under Laura, giving her sister a small shock.

The electricity flowed up through the bushes nearby, stilling the vibration of the branches and the group felt Jaya's power dissipate slightly as many of the plants near them were freed from her control.

"It's coming up from the butte, itself." Mena said.

Bash reached for his revolver, but it was balanced on the ledge where he fell. "Damn."

He looked to the sky wondering what else could go wrong and got a tiny shock from the butte. It was energizing rather than painful, and he was strangely encouraged.

Putting them on guard, he said, "Get ready for

anything because Chuparosa is taking care of its own."

Thomas walked to the edge announcing, "There's something I need to take care of, as well."

"You're leaving us again? Now?" Laura reached for him, grabbing only empty space as he disappeared.

"Lost all of your masters, didn't you?" Jaya put her hand over mouth and giggled, "All you had to do was work my spell."

Laura's eyes narrowed, and she turned slowly to face her. "I hoped it wouldn't come to this," she said quietly, "but we will do it."

Jaya clapped her hands. "It will be marvelous!"

"Yes," Laura smiled, "we even wrote our own ending."

Jaya's head tilted in confusion and Laura drew some lightning from the ground. She played with it in her hands for a few seconds, her smile stretching wider, and then threw it into Jaya's chest, burning off the symbol that made up her piece of the spell.

Screaming with shock, Jaya clutched her smoldering skin with one hand and waved the other to summon more Ocotillo, but the ground shifted, and the plant stopped short of them as Laura formed a line with Mena and Sarah.

If you'd ever asked Mena whether she was jealous of Laura's powers, without missing a beat she would have said, "Absolutely not," and cited the many examples of tragedy that magic had caused the Deane family over the years.

Her powers were wrapped up in her family and friends and she would make any self-sacrifice necessary for those she loved. It was to that end that a week earlier she convinced Laura and Sarah to have part three of the spell — the part they wrote to bridge their powers — tattooed on her upper arm.

The three women joined hands and each of their marks glowed red as they focused their intention on Jaya, who paced in front of them, fuming.

Sarah remembered the words she had spoken to the tumbleweeds that killed Daniel and altered them slightly for her purposes, animating a Cholla cactus and launching microscopic spiny scales that burrowed under Jaya's skin. She cried out in pain and also at the realization that her precious plants could turn on her. It wasn't a necessary part of the spell, but it made Sarah happy.

They closed their eyes and the entire butte began to shake as they spoke the words written in their own language to stop the destruction of their home with a last-minute addition by Laura to avenge Daniel. The hex, taken directly from Brona's spell book, caused Jaya's skin to bubble with hives.

The Bobs flanked Bash and then paced between Drew, Adira, and the witches, ready to fight in any direction. The rainfall eased slightly, and Jaya's face fell.

"You cannot do this to me!"

She raised her arms and shouted commands but the plants around her only shriveled and drooped. She ran at Laura, but her path was blocked by a light so bright that she fell to her knees and covered her eyes. When the light dimmed, everyone hit their knees in disbelief as Thomas tipped his new halo at his daughters.

"Negotiations took a little longer than I expected, but I'm here now, my little abominations, and I'm not leaving until we're done here."

"No," Jaya scrambled away from him, laughing

through her sobs, "it is not possible."

But of her storm, only a few sprinkles fell, plopping loudly in the dirt. She turned in circles like a trapped animal, shouting a mixture of spells and nonsense that the witches easily swatted away. Finally, she calmed and lifted her chin. "I will kill you and start over."

"Like hell you will." Sarah stepped in front of them and used her power to throw Jaya into the white tank. For a moment they thought she'd drowned but then she surfaced, floating on her back and giggling to herself.

"Like Heaven," Thomas corrected, "new zip code, darling — keep up."

"What does she think is so funny?" Mena wondered.

Then Jaya twirled her wrists in the air and the grasses beneath the Bobs wove around their necks, pulling their heads down and cutting off their air. Bash and Drew tried ripping the roots from the ground, but her power over them was holding strong.

"I've had enough." Laura seethed. She pulled as much lightning as she could and fired it into the tank.

Jaya splashed and gurgled as the electrical energy spread through the water, paralyzing her. When her heart finally stopped beating, she floated face down to the top of the tank and the spores carrying the last of her power dissolved from the air.

The plants around them perked up and the group breathed deeply for the first time since they arrived. Thomas flew to the far end of the butte, releasing enough boulders to dam up the flow and halt the damage to Chuparosa. Drew looked over the side and quickly turned away after spotting the flood waters rushing through his house.

When the sun rose over the new dam, reflecting a sparkling glare off the unnaturally still pool, Bash sent out a group text to check on everyone down below.

After the last of his loved ones reported in, he took a second look at the home screen on his phone, pulled Laura into his arms and murmured, "Happy birthday, baby."

Chapter Twenty-Five

Laura was not at all surprised by her birthday party but though she could have won an Oscar for her performance at the door of Isaac's Oasis, her happy tears were genuine. She *was* surprised that nearly half the town showed up for her and that nearly everyone followed Cara's instructions to come in costume as eighties characters.

She and Bash were dressed as Han and Leia, circa Cloud City, and as they made their way through the bar, she was astonished by the creativity of her friends. Those closest to her were still recovering from their recent wounds, but in many cases their injuries had been worked into their outfits.

Sarah complained that Drew favored the metalhead look on a regular basis, so he gave it some extra thought and showed up as Lloyd Dobler. His intent had been to carry a boom box around all night, but his broken wrist made that too cumbersome, so he printed out a picture of one and taped it to his cast.

They approached him and Ben, who had come as

The Greatest American Hero, and asked how things were going after the uproar at the church. Bash felt awful when Ben lost his position as Assistant Pastor, but Drew made him a partner at The New Sanctuary, and they already had big plans.

"I really can't blame Pastor McClane," Ben sighed, "in the two weeks he was away, I managed to get his church possessed by demons."

"So, he's a perfect fit for my church," Drew laughed.

Bash teased, "Nice red pajamas by the way," and left to get some drinks.

Laura spotted Tina and Audi weaving their way through the crowd and poked her elbow into Ben's ribs. He blushed and looked away for a second, then squared his shoulders and asked Tina to dance.

Noah and Brian, dressed as the Blues Brothers, led Laura and Audi to the floor. Audi was still a little weak, but she compensated by acting the sassy part in her Madonna costume. Laura hadn't danced with her son in a long time, and it felt nice to have him to herself for a few minutes.

He'd had a growth spurt and was almost as tall as Bash. With a five o'clock shadow, all remnants of his boyish looks were gone and it made her proud, but sad. He interrupted her thoughts with a grown-up lecture.

"From now on, you have to be completely honest with me about what's going on in town. I mean it, and you better call if you need my help because I don't know what I would do without you, Mom."

"Can I cut in here?" Bash arrived, saving her from bursting into tears in front of Brian and as they danced, she held him so tightly that he lifted her chin with concern.

"Hey, talk to me," one corner of his mouth turned up, "is it dancing to Journey after all these years, or is it something else?"

Giving in to the fact that her emotions would be in overdrive for the next few hours, she shrugged, "I'm so happy that I'll probably be crying all night."

He kissed her and said, "I won't leave your side." Then he raised his head and laughed out loud. "Take a look at those two."

Angie had somehow convinced Doug to go as Teen Wolf and it took every bit of Sebastian's self-control not to howl in their direction. Laura clapped with excitement when she opened Angie's gift. It was an autographed copy of her latest book, The Werewolf's Promise, and she left to show Sarah right away.

Bash winked at Angie and said, "This DJ has a fantastic collection of slow songs."

As if on cue, Toto's Rosanna echoed through the bar and Angie bounced on her heels in front of Doug.

"Do you want to dance with me?"

Doug took her hand and nodded in thanks to Bash for being an excellent wingman.

Sarah intended to stay on the dance floor for as long as Drew could take it. She never got to dance when she was married and was making up for years of disappointing parties. As usual, Drew was happy just to be with her, even though lately they were together all the time.

His house was one of the few that suffered severe damage from the flash flood, so he'd moved in with her and Audi before he had planned to. Daphne quickly made herself at home, and the others were making a slow but happy adjustment.

"We should see what that's all about." Laura led Bash to a table in the corner where Sam and Chuck were deep in a serious conversation.

Bash wasted no time with his questions. "How's Nick?"

After Jaya died, her spell over Nick was broken, but he was already deeply wounded when he met her and his road to recovery would be long. They decided to leave the binding spell intact so they could find him if things went sideways with Sam.

"When can I bring him home?"

Chuck shifted his Indiana Jones whip and said, "You can't have him in your house with Laura, man. Not yet."

She took note that the gun in Sam's Axel Foley costume was real and instinctively looked around for danger.

Sam was impressed by Laura and had no doubt that she could handle Nick, but he didn't want to add to their problems.

"The kid needs medical care, rehab, and therapy...to start with. But don't worry — we'll take good care of him."

He'd never even had a real conversation with Nick, but Bash was, in fact, quite worried about him. Sam and Chuck were right though, and he would give it some time, but he could hardly wait to meet his little brother.

Dressed as John Bender, Thomas attended the party in the shadows, keeping his distance until Rhonda approached him with a glass of Scotch.

"You'll be needing this if you're really planning to stick around."

"It won't be easy for them if I do."

Rhonda threw her head back and laughed, "Compared to what?"

"Daniel kept them at arm's length, and he put them at a disadvantage."

Rhonda had always wondered if there was more to Thomas's motivation when he first sought out his children. Talking to him then, she knew she was right.

"So then...they need you as much as you need them."

* * *

Daniel was buried on top of Shock Butte, and they returned a few weeks later to hold a small vigil in his honor. The witches lit candles when the stones were piled and then everyone stood in a circle around his grave. Adira and Watson joined Laura, Bash, Sarah, Drew, Mena, and Chuck in silent tribute until Drew said aloud what everyone had been thinking.

"All we have to do is read the news to see how easily everything could fall apart."

"It's fallen apart over and over throughout history." Thomas appeared and nearly blinded them with the light from his halo.

"Stop that," Laura scolded.

"Michal's halo is even brighter."

"Yes, but it's annoying when you do it."

He harrumphed at her and turned back to Drew, "You don't have to worry about the news, Preacher. Just worry about who is taking advantage of it."

"Daniel said there are things in Hell that will use this opportunity to cause even more damage."

Thomas placed his hand over his heart. "And I am uniquely qualified to speak on their various villainies. Remember, it's not that simple. In order to wreak havoc on earth they know they have to get by Heaven's Watch."

"So, they'll be coming for us."

"Yes," Thomas's expression was grim, "but we'll be ready when they do."

"We?"

"This team...and me."

"Daniel didn't understand until it was too late. But this," Laura gestured to everyone, "only works because we're much more than a team."

Chuck stepped forward, "And occasional participation is not acceptable, man."

"So," Bash slapped Thomas on the back, "welcome to the family."

Epilogue

After Laura's party, Adam laid in bed reading a news article on his phone. The story was about a vigilante in the sex worker trade downtown.

Cara stepped out of the bathroom and dropped the towel from around her body. "Are you still angry with me?"

"No." He was never angry, but he was deeply concerned for their future. He reached for her and as she snuggled into his chest, he said, "We could have used your help at the church."

She nibbled on his bottom lip. "I was busy helping people who can't help themselves."

Adam was proud of her and who was he to judge anyway? Still, he feared her growing appetite. For the time being, Samuel Parker seemed content to look the other way, but Adam knew they were being carefully watched.

It had been a long, long time since he loved a vampire. Cara was his world, but more and more she was reminding him of how much was at risk. If she lost control, they could be forced from their home. They could lose their friends and even their lives.

About the Author

Vanessa Haney grew up in rural Arizona with, tragically, no access to the Other Side. Had there been a portal, she would have gone through it a long time ago. Instead, she makes a happy life in less rural Arizona with her son Connor, her partner Mike and two black cats named Shadow and Felix. There she writes, hikes and watches way too many horror movies.

Sign up to follow her adventures at:
http://www.vanessahaneywrites.com